THE BOBBSEY TWINS:
THE RED, WHITE AND BLUE
MYSTERY

"I hope I never meet the monster!" says Flossie Bobbsey as weird howls come from a crack in a hillside on the farm of the twins' friends in Virginia. The young detectives not only meet the howler, but catch a thief and discover a special treasure—one of our nation's very first flags. It had been hidden during the Revolution by the young girl who made it. What fun the Bobbseys have in this All-American adventure! They not only solve the mysteries but learn about the early days of our country by visiting the quaint shops and streets of Colonial Williamsburg.

THE BOBBSEY TWINS
By Laura Lee Hope

"Open it quick!" cried Freddie

The Bobbsey Twins: The Red, White and Blue Mystery

By

LAURA LEE HOPE

GROSSET & DUNLAP

A NATIONAL GENERAL COMPANY

Publishers   *New York*

PRINTED IN THE UNITED STATES OF AMERICA
LIBRARY OF CONGRESS CATALOG CARD NO. 79-144071
ISBN: 0-448-08064-8

The Bobbsey Twins: The Red, White and Blue Mystery

CONTENTS

THE BOBBSEY TWINS:
THE RED, WHITE AND BLUE
MYSTERY

CHAPTER I

A WEIRD HOWL

"FREDDIE, you look great!" exclaimed twelve-year-old Bert Bobbsey. "Just like George Washington!"

His six-year-old brother grinned and straightened the big white wig which covered his blond curly hair.

"It does look nice on you," said the pretty young woman in a full pink skirt and a little white cap, who ran the shop. "In the olden days men often wore these." She pointed at the plain and fancy wigs on wooden stands around the little barbershop. "Is this your first visit to Colonial Williamsburg?" she asked with a smile.

"Yes," said Nan, Bert's dark-haired twin, "and it's lots of fun seeing everything the way it used to be long ago."

"We came here to be in the Fourth of July pageant," put in Flossie. She was Freddie's twin.

1

"And to solve a mystery for some friends," Freddie added. "We're detectives."

Just then a long, thin bare arm reached through the window behind him. The hand plucked the wig from the little boy's head and disappeared!

"Hey!" cried Freddie as the others gasped in surprise.

"Stop him!" the pretty shopkeeper exclaimed and ran for the door. The twins dashed out ahead of her.

They looked up and down the street. Tourists strolled past the quaint shops and houses. Here and there were men and women in colonial costumes, who worked in Williamsburg. But the twins saw no one with long, bare arms.

"He must have slipped behind the shop," said Bert.

He quickly climbed over a narrow brick wall at the side of the building and ran around to the rear of it. The other twins followed, but there was no sign of the thief.

The children hurried back to the street. The shopkeeper was standing on the brick sidewalk talking excitedly to several men. They wore knee breeches and white shirts with long, full sleeves. With them was an older woman in a wide blue skirt.

"I'm sorry, but the thief got away," said Nan.

"He took one of our best perukes!" wailed the pretty young woman.

"Your what?" asked Freddie.

"Peruke," Bert repeated. "That's another name for a wig."

"It's the same old story," said a man in brown breeches. The other people nodded. "All we ever see is a long, skinny arm reaching through a window or around a door to steal something."

"That's how the black cape to my costume vanished last week," said the woman in blue. "I was working as a hostess in the Governor's Palace and had it on a chair by the door."

"And one of my little clocks went right out the window," said a stout man in red breeches.

"Almost all the shops have been robbed," remarked another. "This has been going on for two weeks."

"We've nicknamed the thief Long Arms," the woman in blue told the twins, "and we wish somebody would catch him."

"We'll try!" said Bert.

"We love to solve mysteries," Freddie added. "In fact, we're here on another case," he said importantly.

The costumed workers smiled. "Where are your mother and father?" asked the woman in blue.

"Mommy's home in Lakeport," Flossie spoke up. "She couldn't come with us 'cause she's in charge of the Garden Show there. But she'll be here next week to see us in the pageant. We flew down last night with our daddy."

"Daddy's next door at the King's Arms Tavern arranging a party," Freddie told her.

"I'm not now," said a deep voice. "I'm right here." Mr. Bobbsey was a handsome man with a cheerful smile.

Quickly the children explained what had happened. "We don't start pageant rehearsals until next Saturday," added Nan, "so we'll have time to see Williamsburg and catch Long Arms, too."

The four twins had won a contest at their school by writing a poem about the American flag. The prize had been a trip to Colonial Williamsburg to be in a special Fourth of July program.

"We've never had a show like this before," said the clockmaker. "Children are coming from all the original thirteen states to take part."

"We're going to recite our poem," said Flossie.

Her father checked his watch. "We must be going," he said. "It's nearly five o'clock. Our friends will be waiting."

The Bobbseys said good-by and started walking toward the Williamsburg Inn, where they were staying.

"Soon we'll see the Culvers!" Flossie sang out, swinging her little red pocketbook. "Then we're going to Lost River Farm. I can't wait!"

Mr. Bobbsey and Mr. Culver had been friends in college. Last year the Culver family had stayed at the twins' home. This would be the Bobbseys' first visit to the Culver farm.

A few minutes later they started up the circular drive to the Williamsburg Inn. It was a big building which looked something like the White

House in Washington. Three flags flew from a high-pillared balcony above the front porch. "There's the American flag in the middle," said Freddie, "but what are the others?"

"The blue one is the flag of the State of Virginia that we're in," said Bert. "The red banner stands for Colonial Williamsburg."

Just then Flossie saw the Culvers on the porch. "There they are!" she cried.

Flossie raced ahead as a boy and a girl came running from the porch to meet them. They were followed by a broad-shouldered man with glasses.

There was an excited babble of greetings as the two families met and the men shook hands.

"We're so glad you're here!" exclaimed Sally Ann, who was eleven. She had a long blond braid which hung down her back.

"We have a great mystery for you twins to solve!" said her brother Jay, leading the way to a green station wagon at the curb. He was a husky twelve-year-old with short sandy hair like his father's.

"Tell us about it," said Nan eagerly as they all piled into the car.

"Our family owns one of the oldest American flags ever made," said Jay, "but nobody knows where it is."

"My parents think it's buried on our farm," put in Sally Ann. "We want you to help us find it."

"Imagine—one of the very first American flags!" exclaimed Nan.

"That's a great treasure," said Bert.

As Mr. Culver drove out of Williamsburg he explained that his family had lived on Lost River Farm since colonial days. "When I was a boy, I tried to find the flag, and my father and grandfather before me tried, too. But we failed. Now Sally Ann and Jay want to try."

"We have a mystery to tell you about too," said Nan, and mentioned Long Arms's thefts.

"We've heard of him. I'd sure like to catch that man," said Jay.

"Let's work on both cases," Sally Ann suggested. "But the search for the flag will be scary," she warned, " 'cause there's a monster on the farm."

"A monster!" chorused the Bobbseys.

Jay shrugged. "We don't really know *what* it is, but we call it a monster because it makes such weird noises and is big and black."

Freddie and Flossie shivered at the thought.

"How b-big?" the little girl asked nervously.

"Very big," Jay replied.

"Oh," said Freddie, *"that* big. I'll protect you, Floss," he added bravely.

Mr. Culver turned the car into a gravel driveway. Ahead was a gray frame house with heavy vines growing up both sides of the front door. There were long screened porches upstairs and down. On the lawn was an American flag flying from a tall pole.

"You have your own flagpole!" exclaimed Freddie. "That's cool!"

"Yes," said Jay. "Sally Ann and I put up the flag every day and take it down every evening."

"May we do it some time?" asked Flossie eagerly.

"Sure," said Jay as the car stopped. "We'll show you how right now. We always lower the flag before supper. It mustn't be up after the sun goes down, you know—except under very special conditions."

As the children stepped from the car, a slender woman with short, fluffy blond hair ran down the front steps.

"Hello," said Mrs. Culver happily and hugged each of the twins. "I'm so glad to see you!"

After greeting Mr. Bobbsey, she said, "Now let's take down the flag."

The group became quiet and stood in a semicircle around the pole. As Jay and Sally Ann moved forward, Mr. Culver stood straight and put his right hand over his heart. The other watchers did the same.

Jay unwrapped the cord from the holder and slowly lowered the flag. Long before it was down Sally Ann was reaching upward to catch it.

Jay unfastened the clips which held it to the cord. Carefully the two children folded the flag into a triangle.

"You see, the flag must never touch the ground, or water, or anything beneath it," said Sally Ann to the young twins. "You must be 'specially careful to remember that."

"Now let's take down the flag," said Mrs. Culver

"Come on," said her brother. "We'll put it away."

He led the twins into the house. They went up a narrow carpeted stairway to the second floor and into a large room with a big map on one wall. There were two desks, a television set, and shelves full of games and books.

"This is our playroom," said Sally Ann, "and we study here." She placed the flag in a metal box and put it in a desk drawer.

Bert and Nan walked over to the colorful map. It showed a large rectangular area divided into three parts.

"That's Lost River Farm," said Jay.

"Jay drew it," Sally Ann remarked proudly. She pointed to the left section marked CULVER'S FIELD. "This is where you are now," she said. "The other end, Townsend's Field, is where our cousins' house is."

"What's in the center?" asked Bert.

"The original Redfield farm," Jay replied, "where our ancestors lived."

"That's where we think the flag is," said Sally Ann, "—and the monster."

"We'll show you," said Jay.

He took the twins through french doors onto the upstairs porch. He pointed to a sizable brick wall. Over the top the twins could see high weeds and tall, vine-covered trees. It looked wild and gloomy.

"That's where Lost River is," Jay said. "It's really just a large creek which disappears into a low hill. Nobody knows where it finally goes."

Suddenly they heard a thin, unearthly howl.

"Listen!" Sally Ann exclaimed. "It's the monster!"

The children listened, but the strange sound did not come again.

"I don't believe in monsters," said Bert, frowning, "but that certainly doesn't sound like an animal or a person."

"Whatever the thing is, it lives in the underground part of the river," said Sally Ann.

Jay added, "The noise seems to come from a crack in the hillside."

"Once," said his sister, "the monster came out at night. Jay and I were up here on the porch, and we saw it in the moonlight among the trees." She shivered. "It flapped around close to the ground with big black wings."

"I hope I never meet it," said Flossie.

Just then Mrs. Culver called the children to supper.

After they had washed their hands, Jay said, "We'll show you our quick way downstairs."

The twins followed the Culvers back to the far end of the porch. Jay bent down and opened a trap door in the floor. The Bobbseys saw a smooth metal tunnel which sloped downward.

"A slide!" exclaimed Freddie. "That's neat!"

"Daddy had it put in for a fire escape," said Sally Ann.

She gave them each a burlap bag from a basket

in the corner. She and Jay each sat on a sack and whizzed down the tunnel to the side yard. Nan and Freddie followed. Then Flossie crouched on her sack at the edge of the opening.

"Better let me take your pocketbook, Floss," said Bert.

"Okay," she said. Turning quickly to hand it to him, she lost her balance and sat down hard in the tunnel mouth.

"Help!" she cried and zipped backward down the shadowy slide!

CHAPTER II

AN ODD FLAG

"CATCH Flossie!" yelled Bert as his little sister disappeared down the slide.

An instant later she zipped out at the bottom by a honeysuckle bush, head first. Nan and Jay caught her.

"Are you okay, honey?" Nan asked as they lifted the little girl to her feet.

Flossie giggled shakily. "I'm all right," she said, " 'cept I feel dizzy."

Bert eased himself onto the smooth metal, pulling the trap door closed over his head. A moment later he popped out of the slide.

"That was fun!" exclaimed Freddie.

Sally Ann led the twins inside to the dining room where everyone took places at a big round table. After grace had been said, Mrs. Culver served crisp fried chicken with heaps of mashed potatoes, gravy, and salad. The children ate hungrily and did not even think of the mystery until after the ice cream was finished.

"Now we'll show you a picture of our lost flag," Jay told the twins.

The Bobbseys followed him into a large living room furnished with deep, soft chairs and lots of bright-colored cushions. Sally Ann pointed to a painting of two children. It hung over the mantel. "That's Mary Redfield, who made our flag, and her brother John."

The girl in the painting was about thirteen years old and had long blond hair like Sally Ann's. She wore a blue dress and a little white cap and was sewing a star on an American flag. Behind her was a small boy in a red suit, riding a hobbyhorse.

"It's a funny-looking flag," said Flossie. "The stars are in a circle with one in the middle."

"In early times," Jay explained, "there were no rules about where the stars should be placed. People who made flags could put them on any way they wanted."

"There were thirteen stars, of course," added Sally Ann. "One for each of the original states of our country."

"Let me tell you about Mary and John," said Jay. "The Revolution started in 1776. Charles Redfield, the children's father, joined General Washington's army. As the war went on, their mother took the children to France to get them out of danger.

"There is a story handed down in the family,"

Jay went on, "that before they left, Mary put the flag in an iron box and hid it somewhere. She wanted to keep the flag safe from the enemy in case Williamsburg should fall into British hands."

"Why didn't she take it with her?" Flossie asked.

"Because they had to leave in a hurry," replied Sally Ann, "and couldn't carry much with them. They rode horseback to Yorktown where they boarded a French ship."

"Didn't Mary tell anyone where she put the flag?" Nan asked.

"We don't know," said Mrs. Culver. "You see, the war lasted six years. By the time the fighting was over, Mary was a young lady. She married in France and died soon afterward."

"And so did her mother," said Sally Ann.

"What happened to the little boy?" Freddie asked.

"He was sent home to his father and grew up to carry on the family," replied Sally Ann. "He lived in the big house on the Red Farm.

Jay explained that the Redfield farm had always been called the Red Farm for short and that the mansion had been nicknamed the Red House.

"It was burned to the ground during the Civil War," said Sally Ann, "and never rebuilt. Then the Redfields added a field at each end. They built this house and lived here."

"We think the flag might be in the ruins of the Red House," said Jay. "Since it was in an iron box, maybe it wasn't destroyed in the fire."

"Daddy agrees with us," said Sally Ann, "and he's an archaeologist."

"What's an archy-logy?" asked Flossie.

"Arch-ae-ol-ogist," Nan corrected her. "He digs up ancient buildings and pottery and bones and all sorts of old things."

"They're important," said Jay, "because they help us learn how people used to live."

"That's right," said Mr. Culver. He told the twins that he worked for Colonial Williamsburg. "We did a lot of digging to find the original foundations of the buildings here so we could rebuild them the way they once were."

"I hope we find the flag," said Jay. "We promised some of the townspeople, if we found it, we'd give it to Williamsburg to be put on display. The Townsends have agreed to this. They're going to help us search."

Mrs. Culver explained that the Townsends were the only other branch of the Redfield family that was left.

"We hardly know them," said Sally Ann, " 'cause they've lived up North until now."

"The Townsends have handed down the other field from father to son," Mr. Culver said, "while we Culvers have always had this one."

"But we share the Red Farm," added Mrs. Culver.

It was agreed that the children would start the flag search together the next afternoon.

"And plan to stay to supper," urged Mrs. Cul-

ver. "I'll pick you twins up at the Information
Center at one o'clock," she added.

"Mommy's a part-time hostess at Williamsburg," said Sally Ann proudly. "She's working
tomorrow morning. But Daddy's on vacation."

As the guests rose to leave, Mr. Bobbsey invited
the Culvers to have dinner with them two nights
following at the King's Arms Tavern. "Afterward
we'll take you to the Candlelight Concert in the
Governor's Palace," he said.

"Thank you very much," said Mrs. Culver.
"We'd love to come."

Mr. Culver drove the Bobbseys back to the Williamsburg Inn and soon they were asleep. In the
morning they went down to the big, sunny dining
room. A cheerful waiter in a white coat served
them a colonial breakfast of pancakes with butter
balls and blueberry syrup.

As Freddie licked the last sweet bit off his fork,
his father said, "You children will be on your own
this morning. I have an appointment in Yorktown
to meet a lumber dealer." Mr. Bobbsey owned a
lumberyard in Lakeport where they lived.

"You'll be perfectly safe alone," he went on.
"Just stay in the Historic Area of Williamsburg.
It's not very large. You young twins stick with
Nan. I'll see you at the Culvers' house for supper."

Mr. Bobbsey handed each child a ticket for the
exhibition buildings. He gave Bert the guidebook
and a map.

"Let's go to the Capitol first," Nan suggested.

Bert paused and unfolded the map. "We can walk from here easily," he said. "If we should get separated, we'll meet at the gaol—that's jail—near there."

Freddie was looking at the map. "G-A-O-L," he said. "That doesn't spell jail, does it?"

"It's the old-fashioned way to spell it," Bert replied.

Soon the twins were crossing a large lawn toward a big building with two rounded ends and a tall cupola on the roof. On top was a pole with a banner fluttering from it.

"That has stripes like the American flag," said Freddie, "but there's a funny design where the stars should be."

The twins stared, puzzled, at the unfamiliar emblem.

"That's the Grand Union flag," said a voice behind them. The speaker was a pretty girl who worked in one of the colonial shops. "That funny design is a red cross on top of a white one. It stands for England. We fly it here from May 15th to July 4th to celebrate the coming of independence."

Suddenly Flossie exclaimed, "Look! Sheep!" Several white, woolly animals were cropping the long grass. As the girls and Freddie stopped to pet their soft backs, Bert walked on to join the tourists filing into the Capitol. Seeing their brother go inside, the others ran over, too. A smiling hostess in a yellow skirt with hoops underneath appeared at the door and stopped the line.

"No more this time," she said to the trio. "Sorry."

While the others waited, Bert started the tour through the Capitol. When the trip ended, he crossed the street and went into the gaol with a handful of tourists.

A guide costumed as an old-time gaoler told them that Blackbeard's pirates had been among the prisoners in the gloomy place.

"I wouldn't want to be locked up here," thought Bert, noticing the heavy, double-barred windows.

He was glad to get out in the late June sunlight again. As the other people wandered off, he stopped to look at a big wooden frame in the yard.

A blond boy wearing green breeches and a tricorn hat was passing. "That's the pillory," he said, stopping. "People who broke the law had to stand in there for everyone to look at. Want me to put you in?" he added.

Bert grinned. "That would be cool."

The two boys climbed up to the platform, and the blond boy lifted the top board. Bert put his head and wrists in three grooves in the bottom board. Then the other boy lowered the top piece and Bert could not move.

At that instant shouts came from the direction of the Capitol. "Stop thief!" yelled several voices.

"Long Arms!" exclaimed the boy and dashed off.

"Hey, wait!" called Bert. "Get me out of here!" But the boy was gone!

"Get me out of here!" Bert called

Bert shouted again, but there was no one to hear. A minute later a tall man came walking down the other side of the street. He wore blue breeches, a long-sleeved white shirt and a black tricorn hat.

"Help!" Bert yelled. "Let me out!" But the man did not seem to hear and kept on walking.

Meanwhile, Bert's brother and sisters were starting the tour of the Capitol. Just then they heard cries of "Stop thief! He stole my binoculars!" The twins ran outside.

"I'll bet it was Long Arms!" cried Freddie.

Men were running across the lawn while others stood around talking excitedly. The twins listened, then ran to find Bert.

Moments later they saw him in the pillory.

"Get me out! Quick!" their brother called.

"Someone stole a man's binoculars!" said Nan excitedly as she released her twin. "He laid them on a low brick wall and a long, bare arm came over the top and took them away!"

"I hope they catch him," said Bert, then told what had happened to him. "Maybe the blond boy spotted him. If so, he can tell us what he looks like."

"Let's walk toward the Raleigh Tavern," Nan suggested. "We can look for the boy on the way."

At the tavern Bert glanced down a brick walk which led between the white frame buildings to the next street.

"There he goes!" cried Bert. The strange boy was just crossing the far roadway.

"Wait!" the twins called to him. But the boy turned left and was gone!

Bert pulled open the white wooden gate to the walk. With the others at his heels, he raced down the path and out into the far street.

"Bert, look out!" Nan screamed at her twin.

She was too late. Bert ran straight into the path of two huge oxen pulling a heavy cart!

CHAPTER III

THE DIGGING PARTY

AS the other children screamed, Bert darted out of the way of the oncoming oxen.

The driver of the cart gave a sharp command and the huge beasts halted. Then the broad-shouldered man leaned over the edge of the wagon toward Bert.

"That was a very foolish thing to do," he said sternly. "You could have been hurt."

"I'm sorry," Bert answered. "I was chasing someone and didn't see you."

"What kind of oxen are these?" Nan asked as she and the young twins admired the reddish-brown animals with the curved horns.

"Red Devon," the driver replied. "And they weigh one thousand seven hundred and fifty pounds each, and they're only nine years old!"

"Wow!" said Freddie. "I'd hate to have one step on my foot."

Bert had been looking around anxiously. The

boy in green was not in sight. "I was running after a boy who might give us a clue to Long Arms," Bert told the driver.

Just then a small gray bus went past. "Why don't we take a ride on a bus?" Flossie suggested. "If we see the boy in green we can get off and chase him."

"If this man will let us," said Freddie, "I'd rather ride in his cart. If we see the boy, he can let us off."

"I'll do it, if it will help to catch Long Arms," said the driver. "Climb aboard."

The children scrambled into the rear of the cart and settled themselves on some scattered hay. The driver leaned against the dashboard and gave the oxen a short command. The beasts moved forward. It was then that the twins noticed the man had no reins.

"How do you make them do what you want?" asked Bert, amazed.

"They know my commands," the man replied.

"Do you take care of them, too?" asked Flossie. The driver nodded.

As the cart moved slowly along the unpaved street the twins kept watch for the blond boy. He was not in sight.

When they reached the Governor's Palace the oxen plodded onto a long grassy rectangle in front of it.

"This is the Palace Green," said the driver as a group of children came over to the cart. "I have to stay here awhile and let them take pictures."

The twins thanked him for the ride and jumped to the ground. Just then one of the gray buses pulled up near the palace and the children ran to get it.

"No need to hurry," said the smiling driver as they took seats. "I would have waited for you."

The twins thanked him. "Everybody's so friendly in Williamsburg," said Flossie.

"It seems funny to get on a bus and not pay," Freddie remarked.

"We like to make things easy for our visitors," said the driver.

Nan remarked, "It's odd not to see any automobiles on the street."

"Cars are not allowed in the Historic Area during the daytime," the man said, "because, of course, there were no autos in colonial days."

"I saw a two-horse carriage," said Freddie. "I hope we can ride in that sometime."

A recorded voice began to tell what sights could be seen at the next bus stop. Soon the vehicle stopped at the inn and let the children off. They packed a suitcase with "digging" clothes, then boarded another bus which took them to the Information Center.

"We'll eat in the Motor House Cafeteria," said Nan. She led the way to a long brick building with a gift shop at one side. Freddie spied tricorn hats in the window. After lunch they stopped at the shop. Freddie immediately picked up one of the hats. "Boy, this is better than an airplane!" he exclaimed. *"Zzzz!"* Firmly holding it with one hand, he pretended to fly the three-cornered hat.

"I want this one," Flossie put in. She held a similar hat. "It's bee-yoo-ti-ful!"

Nan and Bert each bought one also and wore them to the Information Center.

In the middle of the big building was a large round desk where tickets were sold and questions answered. While the young twins bought post-cards, the older ones examined the archaeology exhibit.

On a board was a drawing which showed the inside of an abandoned well like many found in Williamsburg. Broken plates, glasses, handmade nails, and other items were pasted on the paper.

"These are samples of the things scientists found by digging in the wells," Nan remarked.

Bert read aloud a sign which said that abandoned wells and trash pits could often be spotted by the greener grass which grew over them.

"We'd better go now," said Nan, checking her watch.

They hurried to the end of a covered walkway, where Mrs. Culver had driven up in the station wagon. She was wearing a long red costume with a small, white frilly cap.

She admired their tricorns. "Those were men's hats, you know," she said, smiling. "Mine is for ladies. It's called a butterfly cap."

When they reached the farm, Sally Ann and Jay were waiting on the front steps with digging tools and a big basket. They took the Bobbseys upstairs to change into the blue jeans and shirts and old shoes they had brought. Leaving their tricorns behind, the twins followed the Culvers down to the front hall.

"I've invited the Townsends to supper," Mrs. Culver called as the children headed for the door. "Don't be late."

Each child carried a piece of digging equipment as Jay led the group along the brick wall to an iron gate. He unlocked it with a big black key from his pocket. The gate creaked when he pushed it open, then shut with a click after the children were inside.

"The gate locks by itself," said Sally Ann. She told them that there were four gates, one in each side of the walled garden.

They picked their way deeper and deeper through the high weeds. All around were tall pines heavily draped with honeysuckle vines. The light was dim under them.

"It smells so sweet," said Nan.

"But it's spooky," Flossie whispered.

A short time later the children came out into a large clearing. Jay showed them a corner of pink bricks peeking out of the ground. "Here's where the Red House stood. This is part of the foundation."

Suddenly a sharp whistle sounded. Then three children on a horse came riding out of the trees at the edge of the clearing and stopped. They all had red hair and freckles and carried digging tools.

"Those are the Townsends," said Sally Ann. "We told them about you." She introduced the twins.

"I'm Bud," said the twelve-year-old boy sitting in front.

"I'm Phil," added the shorter one behind him.

"I'm Terry," spoke up a thin little girl in blue jeans who was riding last. She was nine, and a year younger than Phil. "Our horse is called Daisy."

The Townsends jumped down and Phil said, "Let's start digging."

"Wait a minute," Bert called out. "I have an idea. Maybe Mary Redfield hid the box with the flag in an abandoned well or a trash pit. She might have figured the enemy would never look for anything valuable in a dumping place."

Jay nodded. "That makes sense."

"If we could get up high and look over the ground," said Nan, "we might spot a greener place that would show where a pit was located."

"Why would it be greener?" asked Freddie.

"Because," Nan replied, "the things that were thrown away made the earth richer so that grass and weeds grew better there."

"Maybe we could ride around on the horse," Flossie suggested.

"That's a good idea," said Bud.

Jay and the older twins went first. After a few minutes Nan called out, "Look! Near that big oak there's a round spot much greener than the rest."

"Daddy figured the back of the house was about here," Jay remarked, "so that's a good place for a pit."

The three called the other children, who came running with the digging tools. Jay took a pencil and pad from the basket.

"I forgot my compass," he said.

"Use mine," Bud offered. He took one from his pocket and handed it to Jay.

While Jay sketched the location of the spot, the others began clearing away the weeds. After some hard work they had a rectangular section of bare earth.

Using string, Jay and Bert staked the area into small squares. Then each child took a section and began to dig.

"We must sift all the dirt," said Jay. He gave each one a strainer and a box from the basket. "Save everything you find."

The children worked quietly for a while. Suddenly Nan gave a cry. "I've found something!" She held up a small blue-and-white china frog.

"It's Delftware!" exclaimed Sally Ann. "The colonists used lots of that kind of pottery."

"Come on, everybody, dig!" Phil urged.

The children worked harder, and soon Freddie found a brass shoe buckle and Bert the blade of a broken hunting knife.

Finally Flossie sat back on her heels. "I'm tired," she said.

"I've found something!" Nan cried out

"So am I," Terry declared. "Let's go for a ride on Daisy."

"I'll come too," said Freddie.

The three children went over to the plump brown horse dozing under a big oak tree. Terry helped the young twins up. Then she scrambled to the animal's broad back.

"It's funny not to have a saddle or stirrups!" said Flossie.

"You don't need 'em," Terry told her. "Most of the time Daisy just walks. She's pretty old."

Terry flicked the reins several times, and the horse finally plodded off into the woods. Soon the riders came out on the shore of a narrow stream. It flowed into the heavy brush where willows grew out of a low hill.

"This is Lost River," said Terry. She pointed up the bank to a canoe. "That belongs to the Culvers and us. Sometimes we go fishing."

Flossie glanced uneasily upward. The sun was a red ball low in the sky.

"Maybe we ought to go back," she said.

The next moment they heard a low moan which swelled into an unearthly howl. The children sat frozen, but Daisy's ears twitched.

"It's the monster!" whispered Terry.

The howl came again louder. Daisy flung up her head, and raced wildly back into the woods!

"Help!" cried Freddie, as the children bounced this way and that.

CHAPTER IV

MONSTER EYES

THE frightened horse ran through the woods. Freddie and Flossie clung to each other and screamed. Terry tried to rein in the animal, but Daisy only ran faster.

"Help!" Flossie yelled.

When the runaway horse burst into the clearing, the diggers raced toward her. Bud caught Daisy by the bridle, and the boys halted her.

The older girls helped the three riders to the ground. Breathlessly they told what had happened.

"The monster might be on its way here right now!" Freddie exclaimed, looking worried.

"We'd better leave," said Jay. "It's time to take the flag down anyway. The sun's going down."

Quickly the children gathered up their digging tools. The girls put the articles they had found in boxes and placed them in the basket. Then the children headed for the Culver house, leading the still trembling old horse.

After going through the gate, Jay tested it to be sure that the lock had caught. "I wouldn't want the monster coming out of there," he said with a sheepish grin.

"Let's put Daisy in your barn," Phil suggested. "We brought a bag of oats along for her supper."

The Bobbseys followed the others to an old-fashioned gray barn behind the Culver house. After the tools had been put away, the horse was fed.

"Let's dig again tomorrow afternoon," Jay suggested.

"You bet," Bert replied. He asked, "May I help with the flag?"

"Sure," said Jay. "You and I'll take it down this time. Everybody will get a turn."

After the flag had been put away, the children went to wash. The twins changed to their other clothes.

"Leave your jeans here," said Sally Ann to the twins. "You can use them when you come again."

By the time the children came outside Mr. Bobbsey had arrived. Then Mr. and Mrs. Townsend walked in. Like their children, they both had red hair. Mr. Townsend was a big man with a booming voice and liked to tease.

"So we're having dogs for supper?" he asked. "Whose are they this time—Sally Ann's or Jay's? I'll bet Jay's are tougher."

"Oh, stop kidding, Mr. Townsend," Sally Ann pleaded. "We're having *hot* dogs—franks."

The man gave a hearty laugh. "So it's Frank's dogs we're having. When will he be here? I'll get the water ready. Let's see. Do you put a cold dog in hot water or a hot dog in cold water?"

The children burst into giggles. Then Mrs. Culver asked them to help put up the picnic tables and set them. Mrs. Townsend, a plump, friendly woman, carried out bowls of salad greens and baked candied yams.

While the smell of barbecued hamburgers and boiled franks filled the air, the children excitedly told of their finds that afternoon.

"Did you notice a circle of bricks?" asked Mr. Culver.

"You mean the top of a well?" Bert queried. "No. I think we've hit a trash pit." The archaeologist agreed.

"For a while you can dig without help," remarked Mr. Bobbsey. "But when the hole gets deeper, you will need more people. It's too dangerous for you to do it alone."

Afterward the nine children went upstairs. Jay stuck a red pin into his map at the spot where they had found the pit.

Then they went out on the porch and talked about the monster. "There can't really be one," said Jay.

"But we heard those awful howls," Sally Ann argued.

Bert said, "Maybe it's somebody playing a trick on you."

"It can't be," declared Bud. "Nobody has a key to the gates except the Culvers and us."

"Look!" Nan exclaimed. She pointed over the brick wall at the dark farm.

Two green lights were moving along, close to the ground, side by side!

"They're just like eyes!" exclaimed Terry. "It must be the monster!"

"Nan!" said Bert. "Get Dad!"

All the girls dashed inside and called for their parents to come. Moments later, the five grownups hurried onto the upstairs porch.

"Too late," said Bert, as they came outside. "The lights are gone."

The disappointed children told their story.

"I'm sure you saw something," said Mrs. Culver, "but it couldn't have been monster eyes or even real lights. You know yourselves no one but us can get into the Red Farm."

"Somebody could climb the wall, of course," Mr. Culver said, "but why would anyone bother to do that?"

"It was probably fireflies," said Mrs. Townsend.

"Or maybe a raccoon," added Mr. Bobbsey. "You know how their eyes shine green in the dark."

Later, when the guests were ready to leave, the Bobbseys collected their tricorns.

"Oh-oh!" cried Jay suddenly. "I just remembered. I left Bud's compass at the dig site."

Bud grinned. "You want to go back and get it?"

Jay grinned too. "Not now, thanks. I'm taking

no night trips onto the Red Farm till we figure out what that monster is."

A few minutes later Mr. and Mrs. Townsend started up the road with their children and Daisy. After making plans for getting together the next day, the Bobbseys were driven back to the Williamsburg Inn.

The next morning the twins and their father took the gray bus to the Governor's Palace. Before going in they looked up at the odd white animals on top of the gate pillars.

"That's a lion!" said Flossie. "And he's wearing a crown."

"And the other animal is a unicorn," said Bert. It was a horse-like creature with a long horn in the center of its forehead.

"It's a mythical animal," explained Nan to the young twins. "The lion and the unicorn are the insignia for Great Britain."

The Bobbseys went through the gate into the front court. On either side of the big palace was a smaller building.

"This way," called a familiar voice.

In the doorway of the house on the left stood a smiling hostess in a blue-flowered dress and a butterfly cap. It was Mrs. Culver!

After they had greeted one another, she punched their tickets and gave them each a small map of the palace grounds. The Bobbseys went inside and took seats in a room with other tourists. Soon Mrs. Culver came in and began to tell them about the palace. The big building was where the governor had lived. This was the guardhouse.

While she was speaking Nan noticed a stout woman resting in one of the window seats. She had placed her big yellow tote bag on the wide sill.

Suddenly a long, bare arm reached through the open window and the hand moved toward the bag.

"No you don't!" cried Nan. She dashed to the window and grabbed the bag away.

"What!" exclaimed the startled woman.

"It was Long Arms!" said Nan. She plopped the bag into the owner's lap and ran for the door with the other twins behind her.

Nan and Bert dashed around the building while the young twins darted across to the palace gate and looked up and down the road. None of them saw a man with bare arms.

Bert looked at the little drainage gully which ran around the outside of the guardhouse. "He must be a tall fellow to stand in that ditch and be able to reach in the window."

"You saved my bag!" exclaimed the stout woman through the window, and praised Nan for acting so quickly.

By this time the tourists had moved into the palace behind their guide. The twins followed.

On the reception hall mantel Mrs. Culver pointed out a small china object with holes in it. "That's a Chinese cricket cage," she said. "Crickets were considered good luck."

She explained that in eighteenth century Eng-

"No you don't!" said Nan

land and America there were many Chinese and Dutch articles. In one of the dining rooms there were flat wooden cutouts of two people standing in front of the fireplace.

"Those are Dummy Boards," said Mrs. Culver. "Sometimes they were called Silent Companions."

"What were they for?" Freddie asked.

"People kept them in their houses as companions," she replied. "And also so that whenever a host or hostess left the room their guests would have company. It was a Dutch custom. Usually the figures were made in the likenesses of the children who lived in the house."

Nan laughed. "Wouldn't it be fun to have four figures that looked like us twins in our house!"

On the table in the state dining room was a large silver pagoda-like ornament made to hold candied fruits and sweetmeats.

"Oh, it's bee-yoo-ti-ful!" exclaimed Flossie.

Next they went up the wide, polished staircase. At the top Nan noticed a plain, old-fashioned baby gate.

"Some of the governors had children," said Mrs. Culver. "That gate was no doubt used by Patrick Henry's family. He already had a number of children when he became governor, and finally there were seventeen in all."

"That's almost two baseball teams," said Bert with a grin.

Downstairs again, the tour went through the

large ballroom and a supper room trimmed with blue Chinese wallpaper. From there they stepped out the back door and saw the gardens spread before them.

"What smells so sweet?" Flossie asked.

"The boxwood," Mrs. Culver replied.

A few minutes later the Bobbseys thanked her for the interesting tour. She reminded the children that she would meet them at the Craft House at one o'clock.

"I must leave you now, too," the twins' father told them. "I'll see you in the lobby of the inn at half-past four."

After he had gone, Nan consulted her little map of the grounds. "Let's go to the canal," she suggested.

The twins walked through the gardens, admiring the high hedges clipped into tall columns and other fancy shapes. Soon they found themselves in a walled garden with small, odd-looking trees. They grew stretched out on frames.

"What kind of funny plants are these?" asked Flossie.

A husky man with a rake smiled at her.

"They're espalier fruit trees," he said. "It was the fashion to make them grow this way."

"Why?" asked Nan.

"They looked fancier, and the fruit was easier to pick."

"Look!" said Nan. She pointed to a round opening in the brick wall. The children hurried over and peered through. Below them was a pleasant stream with trees along the bank.

"That's the canal," said the gardener.

The children found their way out of the walled garden and went down a terraced embankment. At the far end of the stream was a small wooden bridge.

"Let's see what's there," Bert suggested. He and Freddie ran toward it.

Flossie had stopped at the edge of the water. "Come here, Nan!" she said. "Goldfish!" Dozens of large orange fish swam around the shallow water. On the shore lay a heap of bread crumbs.

"I guess somebody put this out for the birds," Nan said. "Let's feed the fish."

The girls dropped some of the crumbs into the water. The hungry fish rose to take the tiny bits of bread into their little round mouths.

Presently the girls heard a low *woof!* They turned to see a large, skinny hound dog at the top of the terrace. The next moment he bounded down the terrace and leaped on Nan.

With a cry she fell backward into the water!

CHAPTER V

DOG SEARCH

NAN landed in about two inches of water.

"Are you hurt?" cried Flossie, as her sister sat up.

"No," said Nan, giggling. "But I'm all wet."

"I'll help you," Flossie offered.

She laid her little red pocketbook on the ground and started to help Nan out of the canal.

"Be careful of the dog or he'll knock you in, too," said Nan.

The big gray hound was still frisking around the girls. As Nan stepped onto the bank, he seized Flossie's pocketbook in his mouth and bounded up the terrace.

"Come back here!" Flossie demanded, and started after him. But the dog was too fast for her to catch.

Just then the boys ran up to Nan. "We saw you fall in the water," said Bert. "Are you okay?"

"Yes, but I'll have to go back to the inn and change my clothes," she replied. "Flossie can come along with me and we'll meet you boys at the Craft House."

"The dog took my pocketbook!" Flossie said, panting, as she ran back to them.

"Bert and I'll find him," Freddie declared.

Flossie pointed toward the far end of the stream. "He went up the terrace in that direction."

"Okay," said Bert. "Come on, Freddie."

While Nan was wringing out her dripping skirt, the boys ran down the path. Freddie noticed some earthen steps leading up from the creek.

"Let's follow them," he said.

As the brothers strode up the steps, they could hear shouts and laughter ahead. Soon they came to a high, thick hedge of holly, enclosing a large area. The noise was coming from inside.

"What's going on?" Freddie asked.

"That's the maze," said Bert, consulting his small map. "It's a sort of puzzle. Once you get in, it's hard to find your way out. Lots of big eighteenth century gardens had them."

"It sounds like fun," said Freddie. "Let's go in."

"After we find the dog," Bert said.

They passed the entrance and went into the walled fruit garden. The man with the rake was still there.

"Did you see a big gray dog?" Bert asked him.

The gardener nodded. "He went through the far gate."

The boys thanked him and hastened on. They asked several other people and finally a group of children in tricorn hats. They were standing near a long grape arbor.

"A big dog ran in this arbor," a little girl spoke up. "He had something in his mouth."

The brothers hurried inside. They saw a man in costume. He had his back to them and was stooping down examining some of the grapes. Beside him was a big overturned basket.

"Did you see a gray dog in here?" Bert asked breathlessly.

"Yes, sir," the man replied, without looking up. "But he's gone." His voice was very soft and husky.

The boys thanked him and ran out again. They hurried through wide paths with beautiful flowers on either side and down brick walks under shady trees, but the trail was cold.

"Maybe the dog went in the maze," said Freddie. "Let's look."

He and Bert went back to the odd enclosure and entered it. They found themselves walking down narrow passages formed by high, dense hedges.

After taking a few turns, Freddie realized he had lost Bert. Now and then he would meet other boys and girls laughing and calling for their friends. No matter which way Freddie turned he could not get out.

"Bert!" he called. "Where are you?"

"I'm over here," his brother replied. "But I don't know where that is!"

In about ten minutes Freddie found his way out. A few moments later Bert popped out with several other boys.

"It's useless looking for the dog in there," said Bert and glanced at his watch. "We'd better go meet the girls."

They boarded a gray bus and got off in front of the Craft House. It was a large, attractive shop next to the inn. The girls were waiting there. Nan was wearing a fresh blue blouse and skirt.

"Here comes Mrs. Culver!" she exclaimed.

The children greeted their friend eagerly and they got into her car. At once the twins began to tell of their adventures in the governer's garden.

"And did you find the dog?" Mrs. Culver asked Bert.

"No," he replied. "I'm afraid Flossie's pocket-book is gone."

The little girl sighed. "All my 'lowance was in it."

The other twins agreed to give her some of their money.

"I'm not sad anymore," Flossie said.

"After lunch," Mrs. Culver said when they reached the farm, "you children had better begin your detective work. Remember, you must be back at our house by four o'clock so I can take you to the inn." She smiled. "We all have to get ready for your daddy's party tonight."

They ate a snack, then the twins changed to their "digging" clothes. Meanwhile Sally Ann and Jay brought everyone tools from the barn. Together they all hurried to the digging site. The Townsends had not arrived yet.

After a while Jay said, "I don't see Bud's compass." He looked around. "I put it down beside that bush yesterday."

"Maybe he picked it up this morning," Sally Ann said.

But when the Townsends arrived on Daisy a little while later, Bud said he had not searched for the compass.

"We weren't even here today until now," Terry added.

"Let's all look for it," Nan suggested.

After ten minutes of careful search of the whole area around the pit, they had not found the instrument. The Bobbseys and Culvers looked puzzled, but the Townsends were frowning.

"Somebody must have taken it," said Terry.

"But who?" asked Bud. "You know yourself the Culvers and ourselves have the only keys to the Red Farm."

"Maybe the monster was here," Freddie suggested.

"That's crazy," said Bud. "I don't know what that monster is, but I can't believe it's going around in the dark eating compasses."

"You know this is a very big farm," Jay reminded his cousin. "Maybe there's a break in one of the walls and somebody gets in that way."

"Or there may be an overhanging tree," Nan

said. "The person could climb it and drop down from a low branch. Why don't we examine the wall all around?"

"That's a good idea," said Jay, and the others agreed. "We'll take the back wall and the one by our field, and you Townsends take the other two."

"We'll meet you here in an hour," added Sally Ann.

Bud, Phil and Terry scrambled up on Daisy and she ambled off with them.

"If we divide into teams and each take a section of wall," said Bert, "we'll get through quicker."

The rest thought it was a good idea and they did this. Sally Ann and Flossie were back first with Nan and Freddie right behind them.

"Did you find any cracks or openings?" Nan asked, flopping down under a tree at the edge of the clearing.

"No," said Sally Ann. "Did you?"

Nan shook her head.

"I'm hot," complained Flossie.

"That's 'cause there's no breeze," said Sally Ann.

They rested until Bert and Jay appeared and reported no luck. While waiting for the Townsends, the others began digging.

"I've found something!" Flossie cried out. Eagerly she brushed dirt off a small object. "What's this?" she asked, holding up a white stick-like object about three inches long.

"It's a wig curler," said Sally Ann. "They were made of pipe clay. That's a good find, Flossie."

"We saw some in the wig shop," Nan remarked. "Don't you remember, Floss?"

The little girl nodded and giggled. "It seems funny to think somebody used this to put up curls for a man!"

As the girls were laughing, the Townsends rode up on Daisy.

"No luck!" Bud reported as he jumped off. "How about you?"

"Same here," said Bert.

The three redheads frowned, then looked at each other.

"What's the matter?" asked Jay.

"Are you sure you didn't find the compass before we got here?" Bud asked.

"Course not," said Jay. "We told you that."

Phil's face grew red. "If you Culvers or Bobbseys stole it for a joke," he said, "give it back."

Jay answered grimly. "Are you saying we stole your compass? Why, you—"

"Well, somebody did!" declared Terry. "It didn't walk away!"

"Nobody else has keys but you and us," said Phil, "and we know we didn't take it!"

"Wait a minute," Nan broke in. "Somebody else might have picked it up!"

"Let's all look again," put in Sally Ann quickly. "Maybe the wind blew it away."

"Or one of us might have kicked it aside," said Nan. "Come on! Everybody start searching! We'll look for the compass."

"Are you saying we stole your compass?"
Jay asked angrily

For ten minutes the children walked around in circles, scanning the ground. Finally Terry stopped near the oak tree and sighed.

"I'm tired of looking!" She saw a rope hanging from somewhere up in the leafy branches.

"What's that?" she asked. "I don't remember seeing it before."

As the other children turned to look they saw that the rope was swinging slightly.

Terry walked over, took hold of it and pulled. Down came a shower of leaves, dirt and sticks!

"Ugh!" she cried.

At that instant the rope fell and a blue plastic bucket tumbled from the tree. It landed upside down on Terry's head!

CHAPTER VI

PUZZLES

"OW!" cried Terry in a muffled voice.

As she pulled the plastic bucket off her head, the young twins burst into giggles.

"I'm sorry, Terry!" said Flossie. "But you looked so funny!"

Freddie was laughing too hard to say anything. The other children were staring in amazement.

"Where did that bucket come from?" Jay asked.

Terry was red in the face. "You ought to know!" she said angrily.

"What do you mean?" Sally Ann asked. "We didn't have anything to do with it."

"Oh no?" said Bud loudly. "You had plenty of time to set up that trick before we got here."

"Don't be silly," said Nan. "We wouldn't do a thing like that."

Bud was not even listening. "Sure. You Culvers must have gone home and got the bucket and rope.

50

I'll bet you didn't even go around the walls."

"We did so!" said Sally Ann.

"That was a mean trick!" cried Terry.

"We did not do the trick!" declared Jay angrily.

"And I guess you didn't take the compass, either!" put in Bud.

"No, we did not!" replied Jay.

"Come on," said Phil. "It's no use talking to them! Let's go home!"

Terry threw the bucket on the ground, and the trio scrambled onto Daisy's back.

"You'll be sorry!" yelled Bud as they rode off. "We'll get even with you for this!"

As the horse disappeared among the trees, the other children looked at one another gloomily.

"They're awful disagreeable," said Flossie.

"If they knew us better, they'd know we didn't do it," said Sally Ann.

"It's a terrible mix-up," Nan remarked. "I'm sure somebody else comes to this farm. We must find out who he is and how he gets in."

"And why he comes," Bert added.

While discussing the problem, the children dug up several brass shoe buckles and buttons. Then they talked about catching Long Arms. Finally Bert looked at his watch.

"We'd better go back now," he said.

The children gathered up everything, including the bucket and rope, and started home. On the way they took turns looking over the bucket and rope, but learned nothing from them.

Later, though, as Mrs. Culver was driving the twins to the inn, Nan remembered something. She reminded the others that the rope had been swaying back and forth.

"But there was no breeze!" she said.

"That's right," replied Bert. "I'll bet the intruder was right up in the oak tree."

"Wow!" said Freddie. "If he was, he heard everything we said. He knows we're going to try to catch him."

"Why would he play a trick like that?" asked Nan, puzzled.

"Maybe to stir up trouble and keep us from searching for the flag," Bert replied. "Perhaps he wants it himself."

"I don't think anyone but Williamsburg people know about the flag," said Jay. "I can't believe any of them would try to steal it."

His mother frowned. "An intruder would have to use a ladder to climb over those walls. I don't see a grownup going to all that trouble just to play a trick on you. It must be some neighborhood boys."

Before the children could reply, Mrs. Culver drew up to the inn. Thanking her, the twins got out. "We'll see you at the King's Arms Tavern," said Bert, "at seven o'clock."

When the car drove away, Nan said, "We're a little early to meet Daddy. Let's go inside the Craft House and look around." The twins walked to the long, low building.

"What bee-yoo-ti-ful things!" exclaimed Flossie.

On a platform were highly polished colonial chairs and a table set with white china. In the middle was a silver candelabra with tall green candles in it.

"What's that funny-looking scissors?" asked Freddie. He pointed to a small brass tool with a wide, flat blade.

"It's a candle snuffer," said a pleasant voice. The speaker was a woman tourist in a bright-flowered dress. "I just bought one," she said. "In the old days people used them to put out the candle flame."

She showed the twins how the odd blades opened and then closed on the wick to put out the flame. With a smile she walked away.

"Candles were the only light people had in their houses," Bert remarked.

"Let's get Mommy a candle snuffer," said Flossie.

"I think she'd like old-fashioned flowers better," said Nan.

In the rear the children found a Garden Shop with pots of boxwood and packages of seeds.

"Let's get this," said Bert, picking up a large envelope. "These are seeds for old-fashioned flowers like the ones in Williamsburg." The young twins agreed.

After Bert had paid for the package, the children hurried to meet their father in the inn lobby.

He got the keys from the desk and they went to their rooms to dress.

Flossie and Freddie were ready first and skipped up the hall to the lounge. As they went in, the twins saw a row of french doors on the opposite side. They led onto a green lawn. After trying a couple of deep, comfortable chairs they noticed three picture puzzles out on tables, partly finished.

"Let's work one," said Flossie, and they put in a few pieces.

"This is too hard," said Freddie. "Let's have a race!" He led Flossie back to the hallway.

In two places near the lounge the green-carpeted floor sloped slightly. "We'll run down here and pretend we're birds," said Freddie.

Eagerly the twins trotted up the hall. Then flapping their arms like wings, they raced down the two little slopes.

Just then a tall man in a waiter's white coat came from the lounge. He was carrying several cardboard boxes.

"Look out!" yelled Freddie. But it was too late. Both children ran *smack* into the man!

"Yow!" he cried and fell, sitting on the floor, as the twins tumbled over him. The boxes flew into the air and opened, scattering pieces of puzzles all over the hallway.

Breathless, Freddie and Flossie sat up. They were shaken but not hurt. Without a word, the man leaped to his feet, hurried into the lounge and out the french doors.

Just then a young chambermaid came up the hall. "What happened?" she asked. "Are you hurt?" Sheepishly the twins confessed to having caused a little accident.

"I wonder why a waiter was taking out the puzzles," the maid said.

"Maybe the hotel is going to put in new ones," Flossie suggested.

The girl shrugged. "I haven't heard about it." She helped the children pick up the pieces.

Ten minutes later Nan and Bert found the small twins on the floor in the lounge trying to sort the puzzles into their proper boxes. After being told what had happened, they helped with the job.

By the time Mr. Bobbsey came, everything was in order and they walked to the tavern.

"Why do they call it the King's Arms?" asked Freddie. He looked up at the colorful sign over the small porch. "I don't see any arms or hands up there."

"It doesn't mean that kind of arms," replied Bert as they entered the tavern. "The King's Arms were his coat of arms—his sign."

The Culvers were in the candlelit waiting room. A hostess led them to a large table in the first dining room.

"Would you like to eat colonial style?" asked the young waiter. He wore crimson breeches, a white shirt and a sleeveless beige jacket with red trimming on it.

When everyone said yes, he brought huge white

"How many want peanut soup?" the waiter asked

napkins and tied one around each person's neck.

Flossie giggled. "Mine goes down to my knees!"

After lighting the candles on the table, the young man said, "How many want peanut soup?"

"Peanut soup!" exclaimed Freddie.

"I hope there are no shells in it," said Bert with a grin.

The waiter laughed. "No. You'll find it is tan, creamy and tastes a little like bean soup."

Soon delicious dishes were coming one after the other. Everyone ate heartily and finished with plum ice cream.

Afterward, the two families walked slowly to the Governor's Palace. It was dark by the time they got there. Candles were burning in every window of the three-story mansion and in the big glass lantern atop the cupola. Lanterns stood along the walk from the gate to the front door.

"Oh, it's lovely!" exclaimed Nan as they went inside. Polished wood and silver chandeliers gleamed in the light of dozens of candles.

"It's kind of spooky, though," said Flossie. "I guess in olden days people didn't have much light, did they?"

"Not like we do," Nan replied, "but I like to watch the shadows play hide and seek."

On the way to the ballroom, the children peered into a pantry at the foot of the stairs. The musicians were seated there in magnificent satin and brocade costumes. On a table near the door lay a violin in an open case.

"It will be a while before the concert begins," a young hostess told the Bobbseys. "Everyone is invited to explore the mansion."

Eagerly the girls and Freddie followed their parents upstairs, while the older boys headed for the gardens. Jay paused as they were going through the supper room.

"Look!" he exclaimed. On a shelf stood a row of china monkeys, each playing an instrument.

Just then Bert's eye caught a tall man in dark breeches and a white shirt who hurried past carrying a violin. His tricorn hat was tipped down and it was hard to see his face.

"I don't remember any of the musicians being dressed like that," Bert thought.

At the same moment a voice cried out, "Stop thief! My violin!"

Instantly the tall man dashed out the back door!

"Come on!" Jay urged. "It's Long Arms! After him!"

The boys raced down the steps between glowing lanterns into the dark garden. For a while they followed the sound of running footsteps. Outside the maze they stopped to listen. From behind them came the shouts of the pursuers.

"Maybe he's in the maze!" whispered Bert.

"Then we've got him," said Jay. "This is the only way out."

"But there's no use waiting for him," said Bert, "unless we're sure he's inside. You stay here. I'll sneak in and try to spot him."

"You'll never find him," protested Jay. "And it might be dangerous."

"Don't worry," said Bert. "I'll be careful."

He slipped into the maze and tiptoed along the dark paths. Once he thought he heard a footstep nearby. He stopped and listened. Suppose Long Arms sneaked up behind him!

"Jay and I should have stuck together," he thought.

The next moment he heard a dull thud from the other side of the hedge. Something had been dropped onto the ground!

CHAPTER VII

THE OLD ICE HOUSE

BERT'S heart began to pound. Long Arms must be on the other side of the high hedge!

Listening, he heard heavy breathing. Then there was a soft footfall. The man was moving away!

Jay's voice called, "Bert, where are you?"

Instantly there was the sound of running foot-steps behind the hedge. Bert darted to the end of his passage and turned into the next one. Empty! He went this way and that, and finally came out the front of the maze.

Jay was gone, but a minute later he ran from the maze.

"There you are! I got worried about you."

"I wish you hadn't called," said Bert. "You scared off Long Arms."

Jay looked crestfallen.

"Never mind," said Bert. "He may still be in there."

At that moment the other searchers dashed up

to them. Some of the men had flashlights. Quickly Bert explained what had happened.

"Let's search that maze," said Mr. Bobbsey.

"Right," Mr. Culver replied. "Three of you guard the entrance."

The other men entered the puzzling passageways. With the boys' help they checked every corner. There was no sign of the thief.

"He probably sneaked out while I was inside," said Jay unhappily.

"Forget it," Bert urged. "We'll do better another time."

At breakfast the next morning Bert said he wanted to go back to the maze and search for the thing he had heard drop.

"But we've already used our tickets," Nan reminded him.

"Since you're working on a case," said Mr. Bobbsey, "perhaps you can go in without them. I'll phone Ed Culver right now and see about it."

The children waited in the lobby. When Mr. Bobbsey returned he told them they were to give their names at the palace gate and they would be admitted free.

"Also, you are invited to stay overnight at the farm. Mrs. Culver meant to ask you last night, but in all the excitement she forgot it."

"Oh, goody!" said Flossie, clapping her hands.

"She'll pick you up here at two o'clock," her father said. Mr. Bobbsey explained that he had an appointment this morning. "I'll meet you twins here at the inn tomorrow evening at six o'clock."

After saying good-by to their father, the children left the inn.

Flossie and Freddie wanted to go to the mill and the Raleigh Tavern.

"I'll take you," Nan offered, "and we'll meet Bert at the maze."

Freddie and the girls boarded a gray bus to the white frame windmill.

"It looks top-heavy," said Freddie. "Like a tall wooden box resting on short legs. I hope it doesn't fall over!"

On the front were four long, rectangular sails covered with canvas. They were turning in the wind.

"As they go around," Nan explained, "they turn the grinding stones inside the mill."

With a few other early tourists the children climbed the long steps and entered the odd structure. The miller greeted them cheerfully. He explained that the mill was made to revolve on a strong central post which was supported by the legs. "We can turn the whole building so that the sails catch the wind."

After seeing the huge stones which ground the grain, the children went on to the Raleigh Tavern. They presented their tickets to a hostess in a pretty, flowered dress. First she showed the children through the cheerful dining rooms, then took them up a narrow winding staircase to the bedrooms.

"Sometimes two and three men had to sleep in a

bed at one time," she said with a smile. "This," she went on, pointing, "was a camp bed. George Washington used one of these during the Revolution."

The children stared at the round pink canopy over the top of the bed. It set neatly under the sloping roof of the room.

"You see," the woman said, "how nicely a canopy like this would fit under the slanting roof of a tent. Also," she added, "the bed could be taken apart and loaded on horseback."

"Imagine," said Flossie, "carrying your bed around!"

Downstairs again, the hostess said good-by and opened the back door for them.

"Don't forget to visit our bakery," she said, pointing to a long building in the yard.

"Umm, I smell gingerbread!" exclaimed Freddie as they entered. They looked over a counter into a room with huge brick ovens in the wall. Hanging over them were wooden molds including the figure of a dog and a soldier. At a large table a baker was mixing something in a big wooden bowl.

On the counter were rows of small flour bags, gingerbread men with raisin eyes, and bags of cookies.

"We'll take two of the men," said Nan, walking the full length of the counter, "and a bag of cookies."

In the meantime Freddie was eyeing one of the flour bags. It was slightly torn, and white powder was trickling from inside.

"Oops!" Freddie cried out

He strained to reach the bag. Accidentally he poked his finger into it and bored a larger hole. In a split second the bag broke completely and the flour poured on top of Freddie!

"Oops!" the young twin cried out.

Nan turned around startled. At first the baker frowned, but then he had to laugh at the funny sight. The little boy was covered with flour from head to toe!

"If you were Flossie," Nan put in with a shake of her head, "I'd say you were Snow White!" The two girls helped their brother brush off the flour.

Freddie bit his lip and explained what had happened. The baker laughed again and did not scold him.

"Do you make gingerbread dogs and soldiers, too?" Flossie asked the baker.

The man shook his head. "Not now. Years ago those molds were used for many different kinds of breads and cakes."

"I thought we'd take the gingerbread men to Mrs. Culver," said Nan as they left the bakery.

"Who are the cookies for?" Freddie asked.

"Us," said Nan with a smile, and passed the bag around. Munching, the children walked out of the tavern yard and headed for the palace.

Bert had reached the mansion an hour before. As he got off the bus he saw the boy in green coming down the street.

"Hi, there!" Bert exclaimed. "I want to talk to you!"

"Hi yourself!" said the boy eagerly. "I've been hoping to see you around. I wanted to tell you I'm sorry I left you in the pillory. When I came back you were gone."

"It's okay," said Bert. "Did you see anybody that might have been Long Arms?"

"No," the other boy answered. "There was a tall man walking away in a colonial costume, but I don't think he was the thief because he wasn't in a hurry."

"I'll bet I saw him too," said Bert. "Was he wearing blue breeches with a long-sleeved white shirt and a tricorn?"

"Yes."

"He could have been Long Arms," said Bert. "All he had to do was roll down his sleeves after he took the binoculars." Bert added that a tall man in costume had stolen the violin the night before. "We searched the maze for him but had no luck."

"You must be one of the twin detectives I heard about from the shopkeepers," said the boy. "My name is Daniel Coe. I'm a militiaman. I work at the Magazine, where the guns are stored."

Bert gave his name and told Daniel where the Bobbseys were staying. "If you should get a lead on Long Arms," said Bert, "give us a call."

The boy promised. "I'll be watching out for tall guys in costume," he said with a grin and hurried down the street.

A few minutes later Bert was walking quickly

toward the maze. The gardens seemed deserted.

"I'm glad no one else got here first," he thought. "Whatever the intruder dropped must still be there."

He entered the maze and found his way to where he thought the man had stood. Almost at once he spotted a small iron horseshoe on the ground. He picked it up. Stamped into the top were the letters P. W.

"Are these Long Arms's initials?" Bert asked himself. "Was this his lucky piece?"

Carefully Bert explored the whole maze for other clues, but found nothing. When he came out, the other twins were walking toward him.

"Look!" said Bert. He showed the horseshoe and told where he had found it.

"If it is his good luck charm," said Nan, "he may come searching for it."

Bert pointed to a wooded hill behind the maze. "Let's go up there and keep watch for him."

As the children walked around the outside of the holly hedge, Nan offered her twin a gingerbread cookie. While munching it, he told about meeting the boy in green and what he had said.

Reaching the hill, the children started up the tile steps. "What is this place?" asked Flossie.

"It's called the Mount," said Bert. "Underneath is the ice house. In the old days this hill was built to help keep the ice frozen."

"There were no refrigerators, you know," Nan

reminded the young twins. "Ice was cut from the lakes and rivers in winter and stored away for hot weather."

"Pretty neat," Freddie remarked.

The top of the Mount was flat and had a fence around it. There were several benches. One was under an overhanging tree. The children could see far out over the big gardens.

"I think I'll go up in the tree," said Bert. "I can get an even better view from there." He climbed onto a low, heavy limb.

For a while they all kept watch for a tall man in costume. Soon the young twins became restless.

"I'm tired of this," said Freddie. "Flossie, let's look for the entrance to the ice house."

"It's down in back," Nan said, checking her map of the grounds.

The children ducked under the railing and made their way downhill among the trees. They came out onto the narrow path behind the Mount.

"We must be close to the ice house," said Flossie, " 'cause I feel cold air."

The twins walked a few steps and saw a small opening in the base of the hill where there had once been a door.

Inside was a low passage leading down a step to a heavy wooden door with iron hinges. Bending over, Flossie slipped into the tunnel first and opened it. Several feet beyond was a half door to the ice pit.

"We can't go all the way in," said Flossie.

"What's that on the floor?" asked Freddie, staring at a burlap bag.

Flossie picked up the sack, peered into it and gasped. "A violin!" she exclaimed.

"Do you 'spose it's the one that was stolen?" said Freddie. "We'd better take it to Nan and Bert right away."

Grabbing the bag, Freddie turned and made his way up the passage. As he started through the door, a pair of long legs in blue breeches and white stockings suddenly stepped in front of him. A hand snatched the bag.

Before the startled boy could look up, the man shoved him backward. As Freddie stumbled against Flossie, the fellow kicked the heavy door inward.

"Hey!" cried Freddie. "Let us out!"

He pushed against the door. It was open a crack, but would not budge!

CHAPTER VIII

THE RABBIT MAN

"HELP!" cried the young twins.

They pounded on the heavy wooden door. Although open about an inch, it was stuck tight and they could not move the door. The children put their faces close to the crack and again called loudly for help.

"Where are you?" came Nan's voice.

"In the ice house!" Freddie yelled.

Suddenly the door was jerked open. "What happened?" asked Bert. Excitedly the small twins explained.

"We must report this right away," Bert said. "If the man is still on the grounds with the violin, there may be a chance to catch him."

"Right," said Nan. "You and Flossie report to one of the hostesses at the palace. Freddie and I will keep watch here."

Nan posted her brother in the tree over the bench on the Mount. "Whistle if you see anybody suspicious," she said, "and I'll come. I'm going down to check around the canal."

She ran off and in a few minutes was on the small wooden bridge. She peered into trees and brush. There was no sign of a man in blue breeches.

Walking along the opposite bank, she glanced up at the round window in the garden wall. A man in a tricorn hat and white shirt was looking through.

Nan stopped short. *Was he Long Arms?* Whoever he was, his face was in the shadow. As Nan stared, the fellow suddenly pulled back and disappeared. The next moment she heard a loud whistle.

"That's Freddie!" she thought.

Nan raced back across the bridge and bounded up the terrace steps. When she reached the Mount, Freddie was halfway down the steps.

"I saw him!" exclaimed the boy. "He was coming out of the fruit garden!"

"Are you certain he was the man who snatched the violin from you?"

"I'm pretty sure," said Freddie. "I didn't see his face, but he had on blue breeches and he was carrying a burlap bag. He went back of the Mount."

The children hurried around the side of the hill. No one was in sight. They peered cautiously into the ice house passage. It was empty.

Nearby was a long brick wall. "Maybe he climbed over that," said Freddie.

"Whistle if you see anybody suspicious," Nan said

The children looked down and saw a busy roadway below.

"It's sort of a long drop," said Nan, "but since he's tall and has long arms, he could have made it."

Just then they heard Bert calling. In a moment he appeared with Flossie and a slim, dark-haired young man. The stranger carried a camera and looked like a tourist.

"This is Lieutenant Mercer," said Bert. "He's a plainclothesman."

The officer listened carefully as Nan and Freddie told their story.

"It's likely the fellow did go over the wall," Lieutenant Mercer agreed.

"I bet he had a car waiting," said Freddie.

The detective smiled. "You're probably right, young man. You children are doing fine!" After thanking them for their help, he left.

"Did you give him the horseshoe?" Nan asked.

"Yes," replied Bert. "He said it's a souvenir made at the forge. We'll go there and question the blacksmith about it."

"Let's ask about the flag, too," said Nan. "All the people in Williamsburg are familiar with the olden days. They might be able to suggest where it could have been hidden. After all, we're not certain that it's in the trash pit."

After a short walk, the children began to hear clanging which guided them to the forge. The front was wide open and a fire glowed in a big furnace in the wall. The smith, a brawny young man in brown breeches and shirt, was hammering out a small horseshoe on the anvil.

"Do you make many of those?" Bert asked.

"Hundreds," the young man replied cheerfully.

"I guess you wouldn't remember one marked P. W.," said Nan.

"Afraid not," he said, smiling.

"Or a tall man in blue breeches?" said Bert.

"No," he replied. "Sorry. You must be the twin detectives," he added. "Tell me your first names."

Using a small die for each letter, he stamped names into little horseshoes and gave them to the children. They thanked him and offered to pay.

"The shoes are on the house," he said. "They're to bring you good luck in catching Long Arms."

After giving the smith the latest news on the thief, Nan told him about the missing flag.

"I'm afraid I can't help you," he said. "Try next door in the harness shop."

The children did as he suggested. Inside the small white building two men in stained leather aprons and brown caps were working at a long table.

"What are you making?" Freddie asked.

"Leather water buckets," said the younger man.

The older one spoke up. "After we glue the bottom in, we stitch it. Then we wet the leather and fill the bucket full of sand. That holds it in shape while it dries."

Flossie asked, "What did people do with them?"

The leather worker smiled. "Carried water.

They used them on horseback and in and outside the houses. Even firemen carried water that way—in red buckets."

Freddie's eyes sparkled. "I'm going to be a fireman when I grow up," he said. "I have lots of toy engines at home. I could lift this bucket," he added, and grasped the handle of a red one on the window sill. He started to tip it toward him.

"No, no!" cried the young man, and quickly grabbed the bucket. "That has water in it!"

"It has?" exclaimed Freddie, surprised. He peered into the bucket. "It's all black in there and I can't see it."

"The inside is coated with pitch to make it waterproof," the leather worker explained.

While the younger twins were looking around the shop, Bert explained their business to the older craftsman.

"You ought to talk to Elbert Barnes," he said. "His family has been in these parts since colonial days."

The leather worker took a stub of pencil from his pocket and wrote Mr. Barnes's address on an old envelope, which he gave to Bert.

The children said good-by and left the workshop.

"Let's have lunch now," Nan suggested. "Then we'll go to the inn and pack a bag to take to the Culvers'."

The twins walked across the Palace Green and down the street to Chowning's Tavern. After a short wait, they were seated in a shady garden beside the white frame building.

"This tavern is famous for Brunswick stew," said Nan. "I'm going to have that."

"What is it?" asked Flossie.

"It's made with chicken," said Nan, "but in colonial days it often had squirrel meat in it."

"Oo," said Flossie. "I'll take a ham sandwich."

The boys laughed at her and ordered the stew. Soon the hot, fragrant dish arrived with tall mugs of cold milk.

After lunch the children hurried to the inn and packed two overnight bags. The boys carried them to the front porch. Mrs. Culver had just driven up. Sally Ann and Jay were in the back seat.

"Hop in," their mother said with a smile. "What's new in the detective business?" The twins reported their adventures in the Palace Garden.

"You nearly caught Long Arms!" exclaimed Jay.

"He must be getting scared," chimed in Sally Ann.

"We may have a clue to the flag, too," added Nan. "Do you know a man named Elbert Barnes?"

"Do we!" exclaimed Jay. "He's an old friend of ours. We call him Uncle El."

"The Barnes family were friends of the Redfields in colonial days," said Sally Ann. "And their descendants have been friends ever since."

"The Barneses used to have a big plantation near our farm," put in Mrs. Culver, "but they sold it years ago. Now Elbert has a small house of his own. He's a bachelor."

"I guess you've talked to him about the flag," said Nan, disappointed.

"Sure," Jay replied, "but he doesn't know any more than we do. He's lots of fun to visit, though. Let's go see him. May we, Mother?"

"I'll drop you off there," said Mrs. Culver. "But I can't stay. You'll have to walk home."

Soon Mrs. Culver pulled up in front of a small, white frame house with a sign on the fence: ELBERT BARNES—RABBITRY. In the driveway stood a shiny green pickup truck with the same wording.

Beyond it the children could see a long row of hutches and a large shed. As they got out of the station wagon, a short, plump man with round, dark-rimmed spectacles came around the corner of the house.

"Well," he said, beaming. "I have company! How jolly!"

He waved and smiled at Mrs. Culver, who called a greeting as she drove off.

Sally Ann introduced the Bobbseys. "I guess you want to see the rabbits," said Mr. Barnes, hitching up his work trousers. He led the children to the hutches where they admired ten big white rabbits.

"May I show 'em the shed, Uncle El?" asked Jay.

"Sure thing," said Mr. Barnes. "Any time, you know that. It's never locked."

While Flossie and Freddie watched the rabbits, Jay led the others to the wooden shed. "Wait'll you see all the wild stuff in here!" he said.

As he opened the door, the twins stared in amazement. Inside was a tightly packed jumble of furniture, lamp shades, tennis rackets, sleds, old rugs, trunks, and even a canoe.

"How do you get in?" asked Nan, smiling.

"You have to squeeze between the things," Sally Ann replied.

Mr. Barnes had followed them. "Most of this is from our old family home," he remarked. "My sister Sara saved everything from years and years ago. When Sara died she left it all to me. So I just stuck it in here."

"You ought to go through it, Uncle El," said Sally Ann. "Some of those things might be valuable."

Mr. Barnes chuckled. "I don't care about that old junk! I'm too busy with my rabbits. You see if there's anything you want." He walked back to his hutches, leaving the children to explore the shed.

After a while Nan found a child's-sized desk under a torn quilt. "Oh, isn't it darling!" she exclaimed.

"I never noticed it before," said Sally Ann. "Look at the little cubbyholes across the front!"

At that moment the children heard a sharp whistle outside. The three Townsends were riding into the yard on Daisy.

"They look kind of mad," said Bert quietly to Jay.

The twins and the Culvers came out of the shed as Bud reined up in front of it.

"We've been hunting for you," he said, scowling. "We're going to make plenty of trouble for you right now!"

CHAPTER IX

THE STAKEOUT

"YOU Culvers ought to be ashamed of yourselves!" called Terry as she jumped down from the horse.

"You're sneaky!" declared Phil angrily as he and Bud followed Terry.

"Would you mind telling us what you're talking about?" Jay asked. He spoke quietly, but his eyes were snapping with anger.

"You've been digging behind our back, that's what!" declared Bud. "We rode over to the Red Farm this morning, and a lot of earth's been dug up at the trash pit. Did you think we wouldn't see it?"

"I'll bet you Bobbseys put them up to everything," said Phil. "Nothing bad happened until you came!"

Bert's eyes flashed. "You're wrong, Phil. None of us has done a thing to you!"

Terry spoke up. "You promised we could help search for the flag, and now you're trying to keep us from doing it."

"We are not!" declared Sally Ann.

"It's just as much our flag as yours!" put in Phil hotly.

"All right now. Hold it!" came Mr. Barnes's voice as he walked over to them. "I won't have any fighting in my yard. You Townsends came last, so you'd better go now. Come back by yourselves. I don't want all of you here together till your quarrel is settled."

"Okay, Mr. Barnes," said Bud glumly. "We'll see you some other time." The threesome mounted Daisy and rode out of the yard.

Mr. Barnes turned to the others. "Come in the house." The children followed him through the screen door into the kitchen.

"Sit down," said the rabbit keeper. He brought out some ice cream and cookies. While the children ate they told him about Long Arms and the monster.

"I see you have your detective work cut out for you," said Mr. Barnes.

As he dipped up more ice cream for Freddie, there was a scratching sound at the screen door.

"Oh!" exclaimed Flossie. "It's a bunny!"

A large brown rabbit was sitting up on its hind legs, scratching at the door.

"That's Brownie," said Mr. Barnes, going to the

refrigerator. He brought out a piece of lettuce. Meanwhile Sally Ann had opened the door and the rabbit had hopped into the kitchen.

"Brownie's a wild rabbit," said Jay. "Uncle El has tamed him to eat lettuce and carrots from his hand."

"You may feed him," said Mr. Barnes. He gave the young twins the lettuce, which the rabbit ate quickly. Afterward they sat on the floor and petted his long silky ears.

"I'm sorry I can't help you about the flag," said Mr. Barnes, "but I don't know where it is." He smiled at the Bobbseys. "I'd like to do something for you visitors, though. How would you enjoy going on a picnic tomorrow?"

"That would be great," said Bert, and the other children eagerly agreed.

"We'll see if it's okay with our mother," Sally Ann told him.

"I'll take you to Black Point," Mr. Barnes said. "I have to deliver some rabbits near there."

Brownie stood up and hopped to the door. "Let him out, Freddie," said Nan. "He wants to go home."

Freddie opened the screen and the rabbit hopped off the low stoop and across the yard.

"Good-by, Brownie," called Flossie.

"We'd better go, too," said Sally Ann.

The children quickly washed the dishes and spoons and dried them. Then they went into the yard with their host.

Passing the shed, Jay remembered the canoe. "Uncle El," he said, "if you're not using it, may we borrow the canoe?"

"Of course," said Mr. Barnes.

"Thanks a lot," said Jay. "Now that the Bobbseys are here we can use a second canoe for paddling on Lost River."

"Come and get it any time."

While they were talking, Nan spotted a four-seat bicycle stuck up in the rafters.

"Does that old tandem bike still work?" she asked the rabbit man.

"Sure," he said. "I used to ride that with some of my friends years ago. It needs a little fixing up, but it's still good." Suddenly he broke into a grin. "Say, that would be just the thing for you twins! Why don't you borrow it?"

The children laughed. "That would be fun," said Bert.

"Take it now," said Mr. Barnes.

The older boys climbed up onto a chest of drawers, lifted the tandem off the rafters and handed it down to the owner. Mr. Barnes dusted it off, then rolled the bicycle back and forth on the drive.

"Works fine!" he said, beaming. "Hop on!"

The Bobbseys climbed up with Bert in front, Nan in back and the young twins between them. After a wobbly start they straightened out, then rode down the drive and back.

"It's cool!" exclaimed Freddie.

After thanking the rabbit keeper, the children started for Lost River Farm. On the way Jay and Sally Ann took a turn riding with the older twins.

"Let's see how fast this old baby will go," said Bert.

Jay grinned. "Great idea!"

Everyone pedaled madly. Faster and faster they went! Suddenly Bert, who was in front, saw a rut in the road.

"Hang on!" he yelled and the bicycle bounced hard.

"The back wheel!" yelled Freddie. "It's coming off!"

The back wheel spun away. The rear of the bicycle dropped down to the road. It swerved and fell over, dumping the riders into the soft grass at the side of the road.

"Are you hurt?" called Freddie as he and Flossie ran up to the riders.

"I'm okay," said Bert, rubbing his elbow. "I just banged my arm."

"My slacks are torn," said Sally Ann, inspecting a rip in the knee.

"'I'm all right," Nan assured them, dusting off her shorts.

Meanwhile Jay had crossed the road and picked up the wheel. "We can fix this easily," he said.

When the children reached the Culvers' house, Jay hurried into the barn for tools. Sally Ann asked her mother for something to polish the shiny parts of the tandem.

"The back wheel!" yelled Freddie

The girls watched as the boys put the wheel back on securely and checked the other one. Then they all worked together cleaning up the old bicycle. As they scrubbed and polished, the children talked about the strange happenings on the Red Farm.

"I think we ought to have a monster watch there tonight," said Bert.

"That'll be scary," said Sally Ann.

"It's the only way to find out what's going on," Nan reminded her.

When the children finished work they put the tandem in the barn with the Culvers' own bicycles. Then Sally Ann asked her mother for permission to go on the picnic next day. Mrs. Culver said yes.

At suppertime Jay asked his parents if the older children might watch for the monster. Mr. Culver smiled. "I doubt if there is one, but all the same, I'll go with you."

The children packed blankets and flashlights. When it was dark the stakeout party made their way to the dig site. They settled themselves quietly and waited for the intruder. As the hours wore on, the watchers became stiff and bored.

About quarter of ten, Bert sighed. "I guess it's no use," he said.

The five gathered up the gear and made their way back to the house. The girls went up to Sally Ann's room on one side of the playroom and soon were scrambling into bed.

On the other side in Jay's room, Freddie was

sound asleep in the top bunk. Bert climbed into the lower one and Jay took the cot.

But Bert stayed awake. He kept thinking about the mysteries. Finally he got up and went out onto the screened porch. Nan and Sally Ann were there.

"We couldn't sleep," said Nan.

"What's everybody doing out here?" came Jay's sleepy voice as he appeared in the doorway.

Before anyone could answer Bert pointed over the brick wall. "Look!" he exclaimed softly.

Amid the trees the children could see two small green lights moving close to the ground. "Now's our chance to see who it is!" he exclaimed. "Let's go!"

Swiftly and silently the four children dressed in dungarees, shirts and loafers. Sally Ann was ready first. She wrote a note to her parents, telling about the plan, and pushed it under their door.

"If they wake up, they'll know where we went."

The boys were waiting at the slide with flashlights. One by one the children zipped down the dark chute.

"Keep your lights out," said Jay. "We want to sneak up on the intruder."

He led the way to the iron gate and unlocked it. When they entered it swung shut and locked behind them. With the boys in the lead, the children headed toward the place where they had seen the lights.

Suddenly something caught at Nan's shirt. She gasped in fright. Then she saw what had happened.

"Wait!" she whispered. "I'm stuck on a brier."

By the time Sally Ann had freed her, the boys were gone.

"Maybe they went to the dig site," said Nan.

But when the girls reached the moonlit clearing they saw only the long shadow of the big oak.

"Where are they?" Nan whispered.

The next moment a big black shape with wings rose out of the shadows. As the girls screamed, it flapped toward them!

CHAPTER X

A RESCUE

TERRIFIED, Nan and Sally Ann raced across the moonlit grass toward the trees.

"Bert! Jay!" they cried out.

"What is it?" came Bert's voice as he and Jay ran up to them.

"The monster!" gasped Sally Ann. "He's after us!" She pointed toward the dig site.

The boys ran over to the edge of the woods and looked out into the clearing. It was empty.

"But we saw something!" Nan exclaimed. She described the flapping black creature.

"It must have gone into the woods on the other side," said Bert. "Let's try to follow it!"

"I'm scared," said Sally Ann, trembling.

"We'll stick together this time," Bert promised.

Sally Ann grasped Nan's hand tightly, and the two girls followed the boys across the clearing. Near the big oak Jay spotted some broken brush.

"I think it went this way," he whispered.

The children walked on quietly and soon saw more broken shrubbery. Somewhere ahead they heard the snap of twigs.

Bert signaled for silence, and the four children crept forward, following the stealthy sounds. Finally they came out on the moonlit shore of Lost River.

They gasped and froze. A flappy black thing was loping along the bank. The next instant it disappeared under the low-hanging willow trees around the hill.

The children ran over and circled the hill, but saw nothing. The sounds had stopped. As the twins and their friends huddled beside the crack in the hillside, a long, weird howl came from it.

"That's horrible," whispered Nan, shivering. "What do you suppose it is? The monster?"

"Probably," said her twin. "It must have disappeared through a hidden entrance to the underground river. Let's come here before the picnic tomorrow and look for it."

At breakfast the children told what had happened. The young twins listened wide-eyed, but Mr. and Mrs. Culver frowned.

"I don't like the idea of your going out in the middle of the night like that," said Mrs. Culver. "You must not do it again."

"Next time, call me," said Mr. Culver.

After the children had eaten, they hurried to the hill.

"We'll circle it slowly and look under the

branches and shrubs," said Bert. "See if you can find a crack wide enough for a person to squeeze through."

"Listen!" Nan ordered. From deep in the brush came a whimpering noise.

"It's somebody crying!" whispered Sally Ann.

Cautiously Bert pushed aside the willows and saw thick clumps of bushes.

"Ouch!" exclaimed Nan as she tried to move some of the branches aside. "Prickles!" The crying grew louder.

"Thorns or no thorns," said Bert, "we have to find out who's in there."

Pulling the brush apart, he stepped through and Jay followed. The boys struggled forward. Suddenly they saw a piece of red cloth, and a moment later came upon Terry in a red shirt and dungarees. Her face was streaked with tears.

"I'm stuck!" she sobbed.

"Don't worry," said Bert. "We'll get you out."

He and Jay carefully pulled the thorny branches away and guided her to safety.

"Thanks," said Terry, wiping away her tears.

"How did you ever get in there?" Nan asked.

Terry looked at her scratched rescuers. As she opened her mouth to answer, there was a shrill whistle. Without a word she raced down the bank and disappeared into the woods.

"That was Phil's whistle," said Sally Ann. "What do you think she was doing anyway?"

"Same thing we were," said Bert. "She was look-

"I'm stuck!" Terry sobbed

ing for an entrance to the underground stream."

"We better watch out for thorns ourselves," said Flossie.

"Yes," Sally Ann agreed, glancing at her watch. "Anyway, we can't stay any longer. We have to go to Uncle El's house."

The children hurried back, picked up their bicycles and pedaled off. When they turned into Mr. Barnes's drive, he was putting a cage holding two large rabbits into the back of his pickup truck.

"Good morning!" he said. "Climb aboard and let's go!"

The children placed their bicycles in the shed, and hopped into the back of the truck. On the floor were old cushions, a large picnic hamper and some fishing poles.

"Oh, goody!" said Freddie. "I love to fish!"

Jay and Bert fastened the safety gate across the back of the open truck, and Mr. Barnes headed down the tree-lined road.

"Whee, this is fun!" exclaimed Freddie, as the truck bumped along.

Presently Mr. Barnes turned onto the Colonial Highway, and the children saw the brown water of the wide James River on their right. Before long they entered a narrow road which led through the woods. Here and there were signboards with colored pictures on them.

"This is part of the old Jamestown settlement," said Jay. "These pictures show what the people used to do for a living."

Mr. Barnes drove slowly so the visitors could see what had taken place at each spot. There were scenes of brickmaking, tobacco farming, and the manufacture of soap ashes.

"See that sign?" asked Jay. He pointed to a notice on a tree. It named the animals which had lived in the woods in colonial times. Among them was one called an arrachoune.

The children tried repeating the word. "It sounds like raccoon!" said Bert, grinning.

"That's right," said Sally Ann. "This was the old way of spelling it."

"I'm going to show that word to our friends at home," he said, "and see if they can guess what it is."

After a while Mr. Barnes drew up in a wide area and parked. One other car was there—a faded gray jalopy.

"I see Corny Wiggins is here," the rabbit keeper remarked as they all got out of the truck. "I'd know his old jalopy anywhere."

"Who is Corny Wiggins?" asked Freddie.

"He's a sort of handyman who works around this area," Mr. Barnes replied. "He lives somewhere along the James River. I don't know exactly where. Corny's not too fond of work," he added with a smile. "He'd rather fish. Well, come on! Chow time!"

The rabbits in their cage were left in the truck. The children took out the lunch basket and fishing poles and followed Mr. Barnes. He led them among tall trees with a sprinkling of pine needles underfoot.

"This is Black Point," he said. "It sticks out into the James River. It's said to be the place where the English settlers first landed in their three ships."

"I thought that was at Jamestown," Bert spoke up.

"They landed here but settled there," Jay replied. "First they sent out an exploration party in a shallop."

"In a what?" Flossie asked.

"A shallop," said Sally Ann. "That's a small boat which can be sailed or rowed."

The children stepped from among the trees and saw the great river curving around the tip of land. Tall, brown marsh grass grew in patches.

"You can see reproductions of the ships if you go to Jamestown Festival Park," Jay said.

"Anybody want to fish?" asked Mr. Barnes.

"I do!" chorused the older children.

"I want to explore first," said Freddie, and Flossie said she did too.

"Okay," Mr. Barnes answered. "But don't go far. You can walk around the tip of the point and back. We'll be fishing here."

The young twins started off along the edge of the water. "What pretty stones!" exclaimed Flossie, looking down at the wet, gleaming gravel. "Here's a bright red one."

"And a purple one," Freddie added. Soon they

were collecting all colors, even speckled pieces, as they went along.

Rounding the point, they came to a small cove. A man was seated there on an old camp chair, fishing.

"Hello," said Flossie.

The fisherman looked over at the twins. He wore a big floppy straw hat and sunglasses.

"Are you catching anything?" asked Freddie.

"Not yet," the man said in a hoarse voice. "What are you doing here?"

Flossie explained about the picnic, and the fisherman nodded in a friendly way. He asked if they were the twin detectives he had heard about in Williamsburg. Soon the children were telling him about the flag search, the monster and Long Arms.

"So you're looking for Long Arms," said the man. "I'm on his trail, too. I'd like to catch that fellow!"

"I guess everybody would," Freddie remarked.

"I saw him this very morning," the man went on. "While I was over at Glasshouse Point, I saw him snitch a lot of little green glass souvenirs."

"What does he look like?" Flossie asked eagerly.

"I couldn't see his face," the man replied.

"I hope he doesn't come around here," said Freddie. "He might take the rabbits out of Mr. Barnes's truck."

"How long are you staying?" the fisherman asked.

"Until after the Fourth of July," said Flossie.

"We're not sure just 'zactly when we're going home. We'd like to solve the mysteries first."

"I'll bet you would," the man said. He stood up and the children saw that he was very stoop-shouldered.

"Are you leaving?" Freddie asked.

"Yes," the stranger replied, packing up his gear. "There's something I have to do now."

He gave a loud whistle, then started to walk off. The next moment a large, gray hound dog bounded out of the reeds and ran after him.

"He's the dog that took my pocketbook!" exclaimed Flossie.

The young twins ran after the man. "Wait!" cried Freddie. Quickly he explained about the dog and the pocketbook.

The man smiled. "You must be mistaken, children," he said. "Blue here has never been to the Governor's Palace."

Disappointed, the young twins watched the man go toward the parking area with his dog.

"I'm sure it was the same dog," said Flossie. When the twins reached the rest of the picnic party, they told their story.

"That must have been Corny Wiggins," said the rabbit keeper. "His dog is named Blue."

"Did you catch anything?" asked Freddie.

"No," said Bert. "Let's eat!"

When the picnic was over, Mr. Barnes said they had better head for Glasshouse Point. "I want to deliver those rabbits."

Munching candy bars for dessert, the group trooped back toward the parking place. When they reached it, Corny Wiggins' gray jalopy was gone. As Bert opened the back of the pickup truck and started to climb in, he stopped short in surprise.

"Mr. Barnes!" he cried out. "Where are the two rabbits?"

CHAPTER XI

A TALL SHADOW

"MY rabbits! Gone!" exclaimed Mr. Barnes. He shook his head glumly. "I should never have left them in the truck."

"Maybe Long Arms took them," said Flossie.

"Could be. Corny Wiggins told you he was at Glasshouse Point this morning," Nan reminded the others.

Mr. Barnes sighed. "I'll have to go over there and explain to my customer. Everybody hop in!"

The children were driven to another parking area beside a woods. Jay led the way through it to a large building with a high, peaked roof and open sides. Beyond it lay the river.

"Why do they call this a glasshouse?" asked Freddie. "It's not built of glass."

"No. This is where glass is made," said Jay. "The Jamestown settlers had a factory near here. It probably looked very much like this reproduction."

Flossie was gazing upward. "The stuff on the roof looks like marsh grass," she said.

"That's what it is," Jay told her. "The oldtimers used it for roofing on their buildings. It's called thatch."

The children stepped to a rail and looked into a large room with an earthen floor. In the middle stood a low, round oven made of river boulders and clay.

"That looks something like an igloo," Nan remarked.

There were small round openings at intervals with doors. One was open, showing a red hot fire inside.

"Where's the glass?" Freddie asked.

Mr. Barnes beckoned to a thin man in brown breeches and asked him to blow a piece of molten glass on his long pipe. The man stuck one end into the furnace and took out a bubble of melted sand and other ingredients. When the glowing lamp became a little vase, he put it on a table, then came over to the rabbit keeper.

"That's great!" said Bert.

Mr. Barnes introduced the children and told about the theft of the rabbits.

The glassblower shook his head grimly. "I'm not surprised. We think Long Arms was here this morning. A whole tray of small green bottles disappeared from the souvenir counter."

Nan repeated what Corny had said.

The worker nodded. "Corny Wiggins was here

just after we discovered the loss. He told you right."

Mr. Barnes promised to bring the glassblower two more rabbits the next day. Then the visitors left.

They rode back to Mr. Barnes's house. The children thanked him for the picnic and mounted their bicycles.

"Come see me again soon," he said.

Calling good-by, they pedaled off, the twins riding on the tandem. When they reached the Culvers' house, Bert said, "Let's look around Lost River for clues to the monster."

"Great!" Jay agreed.

They hurried to where they had seen the flapping creature the night before. Then, walking along slowly, the children examined the bank of the stream.

Suddenly Bert spotted a small green object on the gravel and picked it up.

"What do you know!" he exclaimed. "Here's a little face on a piece of brass."

"That's very old," said Jay excitedly. "We've seen one like it at Daddy's office."

"It has turned green with age," put in Sally Ann. "Nobody knows exactly what these were used for —probably just decoration."

"It's from the trash pit, I'm sure," said Nan. "The intruder must have dug it up and then dropped it."

"Maybe the reason he comes here," said Bert thoughtfully, "is to find artifacts."

"Could be," said Jay. "There are antique dealers and collectors who buy primitive articles."

"Say, this would explain the digging the Townsends accused us of doing," Bert added.

The children walked back to the house. After Sally Ann had showed the brass face to her mother, she placed it with the other objects found at the trash pit.

Later Mrs. Culver drove the twins back to the inn. Mr. Bobbsey was waiting for them on the porch.

"I know my family has had a great time with you," he said to Mrs. Culver. "It's my turn next. On Sunday I'll take all the children for a surprise trip somewhere."

"And Saturday afternoon we'll go to Jamestown," Mrs. Culver announced.

"Wow-ee!" cried Freddie.

"Why can't we go Saturday morning?" Jay asked.

"Because," Bert replied, "that's when we have our first rehearsal for the pageant."

Flossie hopped with excitement. "I can hardly wait!" she exclaimed.

The Bobbseys went to dress for dinner. It was getting dark when they entered the dining room, and the candles had been lit. A dignified waiter seated the Bobbseys at a table by an open window which overlooked a terrace.

As they were finishing their dessert of pecan pie, Nan suddenly signaled the others. A tall man with a tricorn hat was standing by the window. Instantly he melted into the darkness.

"Come on!" said Bert, jumping up. "That's Long Arms!"

"Right!" Mr. Bobbsey agreed. "Freddie, you and Nan come with me. Bert and Flossie can search together."

Their father spoke briefly to the waiter, then the children hurried outside.

"We'll take the terrace," said Nan.

"Let's go, Floss," Bert urged. "We'll check the halls."

They hurried across the lobby and went down a corridor. Bert stopped at a flight of steps. "Wait here," he told his little sister. "I'll look upstairs."

As Flossie stood gazing around, she noticed a short hall ahead. Back of her in a corner was a large object covered with dark-gray canvas. It was standing on a small platform with wheels.

"It looks like a harp," thought Flossie. She peered under the canvas cover. It was indeed a harp.

Just then the little girl heard footsteps coming from the short corridor behind her. She could see no one, but on the opposite wall was the shadow of a tall man in a tricorn hat. Frightened, Flossie hid under the canvas cover.

The footsteps came closer, stopped, and the next moment the platform moved. Someone was wheeling the harp away!

"What shall I do?" Flossie wondered.

Clinging to the column of the harp, she could feel the platform rolling along swiftly.

"If I call or jump out, Long Arms will catch me!" Flossie thought, terrified.

Suddenly the platform tipped forward as it rolled down the sloping part of the corridor. Flossie bumped against the strings and they gave a loud *twang!*

"There's the harp!" exclaimed a girl's voice. "Where are you going with that?"

"We've been looking for it," a man's voice added.

"I was told to take it for repairs," replied a wheezy voice. "The harp's broken."

"It certainly is not!" exclaimed the girl angrily. "The harp's mine and I'm supposed to be playing it right now."

"Sorry, my mistake," came the wheezy answer. Footsteps hurried away.

"Take it to the dining room," said the girl.

"Wait!" cried Flossie, whipping off the cover of the big instrument.

Beside it was a pretty young woman in a green evening gown. A white-coated waiter stood beside her.

"A little girl!" exclaimed the astonished harpist.

"Flossie, where have you been?" came her father's voice. He and the other twins were hurrying down the hall toward her.

"We've been looking all over for you!" said Nan.

"Wait!" cried Flossie

Flossie explained what had happened.

"I'll bet it was Long Arms," said Bert. "He was trying to steal the harp!"

"And we let him get away!" the waiter said with a groan.

The harpist explained that she kept the instrument in a corridor near the dining room. "Long Arms must have moved it earlier to that other hallway," she said. Bending over, she hugged Flossie. "You saved my harp, dear! We were searching for it in the lounge when we heard the strings twang in the hall."

Excited over her adventure, the little girl could hardly sleep that night. But in the morning she announced, "I'm ready for more 'citement!"

"All right," her father said. "I'll spend the day with you twins. Where would you all like to go?"

There were a dozen suggestions!

He laughed. "We'll do them all," he said.

The Bobbseys visited the bootmaker, the clockmaker, the cabinet maker, and several old private houses.

Best of all, they liked the children's bedroom in the Brush-Everard house. Under the sloping roof was a narrow bed with a blue coverlet. Beside it stood a doll cradle, and a puzzle lay on the floor.

"The pieces are as big as slices of bread!" exclaimed Freddie. "It should be easy!"

Flossie fell in love with a little tea table, set with silver and china. But Nan's eye was caught by a small desk with a matching chair.

"It's exactly like the one in Mr. Barnes's shed," she said. "Do you think that one is as old as this?"

"If it is," said Bert, "it ought to be in a museum. We'll ask Mr. Barnes about it."

When the Bobbseys came outside, the sky was overcast. Nevertheless, they walked to the Market Square, where people were gathering around the green to see the Militia Muster.

The twins noticed a white tent which was pitched in the center of the field, with several cannon drawn up near it. Nearby, on a low standard, was a Grand Union flag.

"Look!" said Freddie.

Across the road in front of the guardhouse was a group of boys dressed as militiamen. Several carried banners, and others had huge drums. A few held wooden fifes.

"What do they do?" asked Freddie.

"A military drill," his father replied. "They fire muskets and march. You'll see."

But the next moment there was a loud crack of thunder and a spatter of rain hit the ground. People cried out in disappointment and scattered.

As the marchers ran for the guardhouse with their drums, fifes and flags, the wind tore across the field. The little tent flapped hard, then suddenly broke loose from its pegs and blew straight at the Bobbseys.

"Watch out!" cried Bert.

But the white folds wrapped around the young twins and swept them across the grass!

CHAPTER XII

FOLLOW THE LANTHORN!

"CATCH it!" screamed Nan.

She raced across the field with Bert and their father after the tossing, tumbling tent with Freddie and Flossie inside.

"Got it!" gasped Bert as he caught the whirling canvas. He and Mr. Bobbsey quickly unwrapped it and helped the young twins to their feet.

When he saw that they were all right, Mr. Bobbsey grinned and said, "How'd you like your ride?"

Flossie looked serious. "It was scary!"

As lightning flashed, a muster boy ran over, holding onto his hat. "I'll take the tent!" he said. "Thanks."

"Daniel!" exclaimed Bert.

"Hi, there!" said the boy, recognizing him. "I was going to call you tonight."

"Do you have a lead on Long Arms?" Bert asked.

"Could be," Daniel replied. "Yesterday a tall

guy in blue breeches and a tricorn came in the Magazine at noon and spent a lot of time looking at guns. Today he was back again at the same time. Maybe it's Long Arms and he's getting ready to steal a couple of boomsticks."

"A couple of what?" asked Freddie.

Daniel grinned. "That's what the Indians called muskets."

At once Freddie said, "I want to carry a boomstick!"

The others laughed, then Nan asked Daniel, "You never saw this man before?"

"No," the boy replied, "and I know most of the people who work here."

"Thanks for the tip," said Bert. "We'll be there tomorrow at twelve."

As the rain began to come down harder, Daniel raced off with the tent. The Bobbseys hurried to the King's Arms Tavern and ducked inside. A loud clap of thunder shook the building and the rain poured down in sheets.

"Let's hope the storm is over by tonight," said Mr. Bobbsey. "I have tickets for the Lanthorn Tour."

Once again the family tied on big napkins and ordered.

"Don't you love this old-fashioned menu," said Nan, "with the small s's looking like f's? I'll have frofted fruit shrub, Virginia ham bak'd in the Approved manner, and Williamsburg Pecan Pye for dessert."

The other children took the same, but Mr. Bobbsey ordered Ramekin of efcalloped *York* River Oyfters.

While waiting for the fruit cup, Freddie spoke up. "You know that building where they keep the old guns—that funny-looking one with the eight sides and the pointed roof?"

Flossie nodded. "Next to the guardhouse."

"Why do they call it a Magazine?" Freddie went on. "A magazine is a kind of book."

"The name comes from an Arabic word which means storehouse," Mr. Bobbsey replied.

"Wow, Dad, you know everything!" said Freddie admiringly.

His father laughed. "Indeed I don't! I looked that up in the dictionary, because I was wondering about it too."

By the time the family finished dinner, the rain had stopped and darkness had fallen. When the Bobbseys reached the courthouse, several people were waiting on the steps to start the tour. A young man in plum-colored breeches arrived carrying three lanthorns. They were made of black iron with glass sides. A candle burned in each one.

"Who wants to carry a lanthorn?" he asked.

"I will," chorused the twins and others.

"All right," said the guide. He handed a light to Nan, another to a tall girl with glasses and the last to a big man with a black mustache.

"First stop will be the Printing Office," the guide told them. "Everybody stick together. We don't want anyone to get lost. These streets are very dark the way they were in the eighteenth century."

He started off and the group hastened along behind him. Turning left, they went down wide steps lit by lanthorns on low standards. At the bottom they crossed a brick courtyard and entered a dimly lit room. A strong, sharp odor hit their noses.

"That's printer's ink," said the guide as he stepped over to a large wooden printing press.

The children looked around curiously at the sample signs hanging on the walls.

"Some words look funny," Freddie remarked. "Sometimes the letter s looks like an f, like on the menu at the King's Arms."

"Yes," the guide said. "And you've noticed that lantern used to be spelled lanthorn. Now," he added, "we'll print something."

From two large wooden trays behind him, he took small metal letters and fitted them into a frame on a flat surface on the printing press. Then he picked up a large round ink pad on a handle and daubed the type with the gooey black stuff.

"This," he said, pointing to a long wooden bar, "is called the devil's tail. Who would like to pull it?"

Everyone laughed. Bert said he would like to. Reaching up on his toes, he grasped the handle and pulled it down. This lowered the paper onto the inky type. Then he raised the lever and the printed paper went up.

The guide held it for the tourists to read.

"It's mostly ads," said Nan, then giggled. "Leather boots one pound."

"They weigh more than that," said Freddie.

"It doesn't mean weight," Nan explained. "A pound is English money."

"Now we'll go to the bindery across the way," the guide said.

While they were crossing the courtyard, Freddie spotted a tall figure in a tricorn hat slipping up the lanthorn-lighted steps. He told Bert, and the boys hurried after him. No one was in sight.

"Long Arms is hiding," Freddie whispered.

"He must know this place well," Bert remarked as the boys went downstairs.

They had missed the bookbinding demonstration, but hurried up the street with the others to the Milliner's Shop.

"Ooh, it smells so good," said Flossie. "Do they put perfume on the hats?"

"That's soap," said the guide, smiling. "It was made in lavender, lemon and bayberry scents." He pointed to a basket of pink, yellow and tan balls on the counter. "We call them washballs."

As the children looked around at the fancy hats in niches and on shelves, the young man explained that the milliner also sold pins, needles, shoes, laces, toys, and many other odds and ends.

"It was a place children loved to come with their mothers," he said.

"And I love it too," Flossie told him. "What kind of hat is that?"

She pointed to a padded band of faded green velvet which fitted around the head. Over the top of it were two crossed strips of the same kind of padding, lined with white leather.

"That's a puddinghead cap," said the guide. "It's called that because of the round shape like a pudding dish. It was worn by tiny tots who were just learning to walk. If they fell and hit their heads, they were protected by the heavy strips."

He grinned. "Now we call anyone who is clumsy or slow a puddinghead. We also have nightcaps for men," the boy added. He showed them a soft flannel cap with flowers on it. Everyone laughed.

"You mean grown-up men wore these in bed?" asked Freddie.

"Sure did," the guide answered, "but not all the nightcaps were this fancy."

"Daddy," said Flossie giggling, "you'd look so funny in one!"

Her father chuckled. "If I ever become bald, I'll get one."

The tourist group followed their guide outside. "Here is our last stop," he said, leading them into another candlelit store. "This is the Apothecary Shop. You may leave your lights by the door." Nan put her lanthorn on the floor with the others.

"You are in an old-fashioned drugstore," the guide went on. "The doctor had his office in the back room and sold medicines here in the front."

The boy pointed out huge green glass bottles and showed them a small tool for making pills. Then he led them into the office to see the doctor's big slant-top desk and instruments.

Nan and Freddie were first to come back into the shop. They stopped short and gasped. A long bare arm was disappearing around the doorway with one of the lanthorns!

"Long Arms!" exclaimed Freddie.

"We mustn't let him get away!" Nan cried.

She dashed from the shop with Freddie. The man was racing up the street swinging the lanthorn. He darted into the walkway beside the Raleigh Tavern. By the time the two children reached it, the light was across the next street.

Running hard, the Bobbseys tried to catch up. They went through gardens and down side streets, but the lanthorn was always well ahead. Finally it vanished.

Nan stamped her foot crossly. "Lost him again!" she cried in disappointment. "Well, let's go back."

"Which way?" Freddie asked.

Nan had to confess she did not know. "I guess we're lost."

As the two tried to remember how they had come, a large man with a lanthorn suddenly stepped from a garden walk.

"Where do you think you're going?" he asked.

For a moment the children were too frightened to answer. Then they recognized him. He was one of the men from their tour!

"Everybody's looking for you," he said, and led them back to the Apothecary Shop.

"Where do you think you're going?"
the man asked gruffly

A few minutes later Mr. Bobbsey arrived with the other twins and several men who had been searching for Nan and Freddie.

"You must not run off again," he told them.

Nan and Freddie apologized and explained about chasing Long Arms. When the Bobbseys reached the inn, Bert telephoned Jay and reported what Daniel had told him. It was arranged that the Culver children would meet the twins the next noon at the Magazine.

"And catch Long Arms!" Freddie shouted.

"We go to rehearsal in the morning," Flossie reminded him.

Mr. Bobbsey said, "I spoke to the director of the pageant. You're to report at nine o'clock to the Wren Building at the College of William and Mary."

Flossie looked puzzled. "How can we practice in a birdhouse?"

Mr. Bobbsey laughed. "It's not a birdhouse. It's a building designed by a famous English architect named Christopher Wren. The College of William and Mary is the second oldest in the United States," he added.

Next morning the Bobbseys arrived promptly at a large rosy brick building with a cupola. A dozen small groups of children had gathered on the wide lawn.

The muster boys were at one side with their flags and drums. The twins spotted Daniel, who waved to them.

The director of the pageant, a handsome young man with a loud voice, gave the groups their positions. "Your costumes will be a secret until the big day," he said. "Don't tell anyone except your family."

Each person was given a slip of paper. When Flossie read hers, she jumped up and down. "Oh, I just love mine!"

The rehearsal ended late in the morning. Immediately the twins hurried with Daniel to the Magazine.

"It's nearly twelve," said Nan. "We don't want to miss Long Arms."

When they reached the green in front of the building, they saw the Culver children with a group of tourists. They were watching a young man demonstrate an old musket. The Bobbseys hurried over to them.

"Now everybody count," said the guide, pointing the gun straight up in the air.

"One-two-three-fire!" shouted the tourists.

BANG! The old gun went off, sending up a puff of smoke.

As the children turned away laughing and talking, Bert saw a tall man in blue breeches come out of the Magazine. He wore a tricorn and carried two muskets.

"There he is!" cried Bert.

The six children dashed across the grass and formed a circle around the surprised man.

"We've got you, Long Arms!" cried Freddie.

CHAPTER XIII

A WELL-KEPT SECRET

THE tall man looked down at the excited children and laughed. "I'm afraid you've made a mistake. I'm not Long Arms."

"I'll say he's not!" came a cheerful voice.

"Lieutenant Mercer!" exclaimed Bert. The twins recognized the plainclothesman who had talked to them in the Palace Garden.

"I'll have to tell you a secret," Lieutenant Mercer said quietly. "This is Mike Lasalle, one of our detectives."

The children looked embarrassed. "We're sorry," said Nan, "but when we saw you come out with the muskets we thought you were the thief."

"It's all right." Mike Lasalle smiled. He explained that old firearms were his hobby. "For the past two days I've come here on my lunch hour to look over the guns in the Magazine. Today I brought two of my own to compare with them."

"You must be new on the job," put in Daniel, who had come over to listen.

"I've been here three days."

Bert told the two men all that had happened since he had found the horseshoe.

"We haven't done any better," admitted Lieutenant Mercer. He wished the children luck and they parted.

"We have half an hour to wait before we meet Mother at the inn," said Sally Ann.

"Let's go to the Silversmith's Shop," Bert suggested.

Sally Ann spoke up. "Jay and I have been there before. We'll meet you at the Milliner's. Mother wants some washballs."

The twins gave their tickets to the white-haired hostess at the silversmith's house. After showing them the dwelling, she led the twins into an adjoining office.

"This is where the silversmith kept his accounts," she said. "On the other side of this room is his shop." She smiled. "Making silver ornaments is a very noisy business, so it was a good idea to have the office between his house and the shop. Then the family wasn't bothered by the sound of the hammering."

The children went through and found themselves in a light, airy room with a counter across the front facing the street door. Behind it was a big wooden block with a heavy mallet lying on it.

Nailed to one wall was a glass case full of beautifully polished silver objects.

A young man came from the back with a large piece of silver shaped roughly like a basin.

"Hello," he said cheerfully, and put the article on a round mold on the block. "I'm going to beat this into a bowl," he said, "so you'd better hold your ears."

As he raised the mallet his glance fell on the counter. "Oh-oh!" he said with a frown, and lowered the hammer. He gave a quick look around the room. "What happened to all the silver that was on the counter?"

The tourists looked surprised.

"Nothing was there when we came in," said Nan.

The apprentice turned pale. "But I was gone only a few minutes! There were two teaspoons, a candle snuffer and a small bowl. Are you sure you didn't see them?"

Everyone said no. "I'll bet Long Arms took them!" Bert spoke up.

The twins ran outside and looked up and down the street and around the corner, but saw no tall man in a tricorn. When they went back the young man was talking excitedly to an older craftsman.

"Nothing we can do but report it," said the older man. He looked sad. "I certainly hope someone catches that thief soon!"

As the children walked toward the Milliner's

Shop, Freddie said, "How does Long Arms get away?"

"There are so many men in costume," answered Nan, "that no one notices him. Even if he's carrying something like a burlap bag or a lanthorn, who would pay attention?"

"No one," Bert agreed. "People would just think it was part of his job."

The Culvers were waiting outside the Milliner's Shop. As the children walked toward the inn, the Bobbseys told about the theft. They repeated the story a short time later when Mrs. Culver drove up in the station wagon.

"That's too bad," she said, "but let's forget about Long Arms now and have lunch."

After stopping along the road for hamburgers, french fried potatoes and cold soda, they drove on. As they approached Jamestown Island, Jay pointed out a long wall built along the shore.

"The land was gradually being washed away into the river," he explained. "The concrete barrier was put up to keep from losing any more."

Sally Ann added, "The fort built by the first settlers was probably on that part of the island which is underwater now. But there are lots of foundations of houses, and part of the church is still standing."

Mrs. Culver parked in a large lot, and they walked across a wooden bridge to the Visitor Center.

"Look who's here!" said Nan. "I think it's the dog who knocked me into the water!"

Outside the building sat a big gray hound. He was leashed to a ring on a wooden figure of a dog.

"Isn't that cute!" said Flossie. It's a doggie parking station." She patted the hound, who gave a friendly woof.

"He could be Corny Wiggins' dog," said Freddie. "And if he's here, that might mean that Long Arms is too. Corny said he was on his trail."

"We'll keep our eyes open for both of them," Bert declared. "Even if we don't see the thief, maybe Corny Wiggins could give us a clue."

The group walked into the park and looked at the ruins of brick foundations. Here and there were white brick boxes with green loudspeakers set into them.

"Listen!" said Sally Ann.

She pushed a red button on one, and a recorded voice told about the house which had stood on the spot.

For over an hour the twins and Culvers strolled around. They visited the old church and the graveyard where many colonists were buried.

"The settlers here had a hard time of it," said Mrs. Culver. "They were not used to such a wilderness. They didn't have enough food and became ill. The second year was so bad they even had to eat snakes and lizards."

"Ugh!" said Flossie and everybody shivered.

"A few managed to survive," Mrs. Culver went

"It's a doggie parking station,"
said Flossie

on. "Finally help came from England and the colony was saved."

"They must have been very brave," said Freddie, and the others agreed. By now they had returned to the Visitor Center.

"Blue is gone—if it was Blue," said Flossie. "Corny must have left."

The group went inside to buy postcards. While paying for them, they heard one clerk say to another that a whole box of souvenir key chains was missing.

"Somebody must have taken them," replied the first clerk. "I just put them out on the counter a little while ago."

"Long Arms probably was here," Nan whispered when she was outside again. The children looked around for the thief but saw no one who seemed likely.

"Now we'll go to Jamestown Festival Park," said Mrs. Culver as they climbed into the car. "You'll see reproductions of the original fort, the three ships and an Indian lodge."

"An Indian lodge! Whee!" said Freddie.

When they reached the park, Mrs. Culver said she would wait in the snack shop. "I've seen the exhibit many times," she remarked.

The children hastened down the wide path to a long, round-topped dwelling made of reeds. Inside sat an Indian with piles of furs around him.

"This was the kind of house the Indian Chief Powhatan lived in," said Jay.

Freddie wanted to clap his hand to his mouth and give an Indian war whoop but politely kept still. Besides, he knew that today Indians do not do this.

The children hurried on and went through the large three-sided fort made of logs. What they wanted to see most were the three brightly colored ships which lay at anchor straight ahead.

"They're so little!" said Nan.

"The settlers came all the way across the ocean in *those?*" exclaimed Bert.

"They're not very big compared to our ships today," said Jay, "but they carried 105 men and boys and three goats."

"You can go aboard the *Susan Constant,*" said Sally Ann. "That's the biggest. She was the flagship."

When the children reached the gangplank, they saw the Townsend children standing at the top of it. Before anyone could speak, Bud ran down and shoved Jay backward.

"Hey, cut it out!" exclaimed Jay angrily.

"That's for sneaking poor old Daisy out of our barn and racing her up the road and leaving her in a field!" said Bud.

"We went looking for her when she was missing," put in Terry, "and we found her all shaking and scared."

"And we didn't like the sign you put around her neck either! We will *not* stay out of the Red Farm! It's as much ours as it is yours!" shouted Phil.

"But we didn't do it!" declared Sally Ann.

Bud gave Jay another hard push, and Jay pushed back.

"Knock it off!" ordered a broad-shouldered young man in a settler's costume. "Stop the fighting or get out!"

The Townsends scowled and ran away. The others went back to the snack shop. Mrs. Culver was waiting at the door. She looked worried.

"I met Mrs. Townsend inside," she said, "and had a soda with her. She told me about the horse."

"Mother, you know we'd never hurt Daisy," said Jay. "Somebody else is pulling these tricks."

"Yes," his mother agreed. "Mrs. Townsend and I both believe that. We must get to the bottom of this mystery."

Later, while she prepared supper, the children pedaled to Mr. Barnes's to look at his old desk. He was glad to see them.

Nan explained about the desk in the Brush-Everard house, and asked, "Is the one in your shed very old?"

"I don't know," he said. "Let's look it over."

The boys went into the shed and brought the child's desk out onto the drive.

"Here's a label," said Sally Ann. A square of paper with writing on it was pasted to the back.

"That's my sister's handwriting," said Mr. Barnes. "What does it say?"

Bert read aloud: "This is one of the toys given

by the Redfield family to the Barnes children in 1783."

Nan's eyes grew wide in excitement. "1783—that was right after the Revolutionary War ended! This desk must have belonged to Mary Redfield."

"Of course!" exclaimed Sally Ann. "John was too young for it."

"And when he came back," Nan went on, "he would have been too old for the desk, so it was given away!"

"Oh, if only this little desk could talk!" exclaimed Sally Ann. "It could probably tell us where the flag is!"

Nan had been carefully examining the dark, polished wood. She felt gently in each pigeonhole. Suddenly there was a squeaky sound and the whole row of them swung out.

"A secret compartment!" Flossie exclaimed.

"And there's a paper in it!" Bert added.

CHAPTER XIV

A SLIPPERY DISCOVERY

EXCITEDLY Nan took the note from the hidden compartment of the little desk.

"What does it say?" Bert asked as his sister carefully unfolded the old, yellowed paper.

"It says, 'I hid the flag inside John's Little Gray,' and it's signed, 'Mary.'"

Sally Ann squealed in delight. "From Mary Redfield! To think she wrote this herself nearly two hundred years ago!"

"It's great," said Jay. "But what does it mean? The flag is inside John's little gray—his little gray *what?*"

Bert examined the note. "The words little and gray are capitalized," he said. "Maybe they are the name of something."

Mr. Barnes puzzled over the message too, but could not guess what it meant.

"Take the note home," he said to Jay, "and show it to your father. He knows all about the olden days. Maybe he'll be able to figure out the meaning."

Half an hour later the children gave the paper to Mr. Culver. He exclaimed in delight, "This is fabulous!"

However, neither he nor Mrs. Culver could figure out what the note meant.

"I don't understand why Mary hid it," said Sally Ann. "Why didn't she just tell somebody her secret?"

"Maybe," said Nan, "she didn't want anyone on the farm to know it, because he might tell the enemy."

Mr. Culver carefully placed the yellowed paper in a heavy brown envelope and sealed it. "I will take this to my office," he said, "and put it away safely."

Just before supper Mr. Bobbsey arrived in his rented car. Excitedly the twins told him about the note.

"That's great!" he said. "It looks as if you detectives are making real progress!"

Later, as they were leaving, Mrs. Culver reminded the Bobbseys that the next day was Sunday. "Let's all go to church together in Williamsburg," she suggested.

"Good idea," said Mr. Bobbsey. He suggested that Sally Ann and Jay pack a bag of play clothes for the next day. "I'll take it to the inn and you can change there."

"Tomorrow is Surprise Day!" said Flossie.

The next morning she and Nan put on neat blue dresses with white gloves, purses and straw hats. The boys wore gray suits. When they reached the old brick church, the Culvers were waiting. Sally Ann had on a pink dress with a white hat and gloves.

"This is Bruton Parish Church," said Mrs. Culver as the Bobbseys approached the door. "It has been in use since 1715. George Washington and many other patriots worshipped here."

Inside, the children were surprised to see that the white wooden sides of the pews were very high. When seated, Flossie and Freddie could barely see over the top.

"The pews were enclosed like this to keep the people warm," Mrs. Culver explained quietly. "Back in those times the churches weren't heated."

After the service, Mr. and Mrs. Culver said good-by and left. The others hurried to the inn and changed clothes. When the six children came out in shirts and shorts, Mr. Bobbsey was waiting at the door with the station wagon. There was something box-shaped in back covered by a large blanket.

"What's that?" Freddie asked.

"A surprise."

"Where are we going, Daddy?" Flossie asked.

"You'll see," Mr. Bobbsey answered with a grin.

After a while a sparkling blue river appeared on their right.

"I know, I bet," said Jay. "Yorktown! That's the York River!"

A few minutes later they rode into a wide open area of low rolling hills.

"I was right!" Jay exclaimed.

"This is the battlefield where the Colonists fought the last great battle against England," Sally Ann told the twins. "When the British surrendered here it meant that America had won her independence."

Mr. Bobbsey parked at the Visitor Center and they all went inside to see colored slides about the Revolution. Music played, and a voice told the story. One of the pictures showed a British drummer boy carrying a white flag of truce on a sword.

"That flag was the signal that the British were willing to talk over peace terms," said Bert softly to Freddie. "Drummers were very important in the Army. They sounded many kinds of signals, and of course they played in the band."

"I'd like to be a drummer boy," said Freddie.

"Instead of a fireman?" Bert teased.

"Well, I'll see," Freddie answered.

After the show the visitors went downstairs and walked through a replica of a British gunboat.

"This was the gundeck," said Mr. Bobbsey when they entered a room dimly lit by lanterns. He had to bend his head to go under the low, heavy beams.

"The British had lots of boats out in Yorktown Harbor," said Jay, "but the French fleet destroyed them."

"France helped America win her independence," Nan explained to the little twins.

From the Visitor Center Mr. Bobbsey drove slowly around the huge battlefield, and finally down a lonely dirt lane.

"This is Surrender Road," said Jay. He pointed to a grassy area on their left. "And that's Surrender Field. The British Army marched along here and went into the field to lay down their muskets."

Sally Ann added, "And their band played a song called 'The World Turned Upside Down.'"

Bert chuckled. "I guess the world did seem topsy-turvy to the English that day. After all, England was an old, strong country and we were young and weak."

"But we won!" cried Freddie proudly.

Mr. Bobbsey drove back toward Jamestown and parked beside a large creek near a bridge.

"Now we'll have our picnic," he said. "Look under the blanket."

Eagerly the children lifted the covering and found a large picnic hamper. Beside it was a pile of kites.

"Oh, they're bee-yoo-ti-ful!" exclaimed Flossie as Nan took them out. The kites were in odd shapes and bright colors.

"There's a polka-dot fish!" exclaimed Freddie.

At one he grasped the string and began to run. The kite lifted into the air.

In his excitement Freddie did not watch where he was going. Suddenly he stumbled over a rock.

Freddie let go of the string and sprawled on the ground. The kite flew away.

As the little boy picked himself up, there were tears in his eyes. Nan had rushed up to him.

"Never mind, honey," she said. "You may have my kite. It has a clown face on it."

Freddie felt better and joined the others, who were ready to eat the southern fried chicken, ham sandwiches and ice cream. Afterward the children flew the kites but when the breeze died down, they gave it up.

"Let's walk along the bank," Bert suggested.

He put the kites in the station wagon, and the group separated. Bert, Freddie and Jay went single file in one direction. The water was almost covered by green lily pads. Among them were large heaps of brown brush.

"What are those?" Bert asked.

"Muskrat mounds," said Jay. He explained that the furry animals with their ratlike tails built the mounds of cattails. "They're hollow inside," Jay explained. "That's where the muskrats hide and have their nests."

"Oh, look at the turtle!" Freddie exclaimed.

On a lily pad near a mound was a small dark green turtle, sunning himself.

"I wish we could catch him," said Freddie. "Is it deep there?"

"I don't think so," said Jay. "Muskrats usually make their mounds in shallow water."

"You can't keep him, you know, Freddie," said

Bert. "It isn't fair to take him away from his home and coop him up in a pen."

"I know," said Freddie. "I just want to hold him a little while."

"Okay," said Bert. "Let's try to capture him!"

The three boys took off their sandals and started to wade quietly toward the dozing turtle.

"Wow! The ground's squishy and slippery!" said Freddie. Soon the water reached the edge of his shorts.

"Wait here," said Bert. He went on with Jay behind him. When they were beside the mound Jay whispered, "Stop here. If you go any closer he might see you and dive off."

As Bert reached cautiously toward the creature, his foot slipped on the bottom. With a yell, he fell sideways and grabbed the muskrat mound for support. At the same time the turtle slid off the lily pad and swam away.

"Watch out!" exclaimed Freddie as Jay steadied Bert. "The muskrat might come out!"

But nothing happened. The tilted nest remained quiet. As Bert tried to straighten it, something shiny caught his eye. Cautiously he put his hand in and brought out a silver candle snuffer. The boys stared in amazement.

"It has the Williamsburg mark on it," Jay cried out. "This is part of the stolen silver!"

Bert slid his hand inside the nest again. This time he felt cloth and pulled out a little bag. It was full of small silver pieces.

"Part of the stolen silver!" Bert cried out

"Take it to shore, Jay," said Bert, handing it to his friend. "I'll put this nest back together again." When the muskrat's home was repaired, Bert hastened after Jay and Freddie, who were showing their discovery to the others.

"Long Arms must have hidden these in the mound," said Nan. "Maybe there are things in the other nests too."

"We'll leave that for the police to find out," said her father. "We must take this loot back to Williamsburg at once."

An hour later he and the children were in the manager's office of the inn with Lieutenant Mercer. The officer listened carefully to their story, then congratulated the children on their discovery.

"We'll have the mounds searched," he promised.

By evening the story was on the local radio, and everyone in the hotel had heard of the young detectives.

As the girls were getting ready for bed, Nan said, "Long Arms must know by now that we found his hiding place. He'll be extra careful from now on."

"We'd better be careful too," said Sally Ann, " 'cause he must be very mad at us."

Next morning the little twins were dressed first. As they walked into the lobby, a bellboy came up to them and said, "How's your detective work this morning?"

The twins beamed and blushed. "We're working on another case too," said Freddie importantly. "It's about a flag."

Flossie's eyes sparkled with fun. She had just made up a verse! "Yes," she said, "but we still need a clue to the red, white and blue!"

The bellboy laughed. "I'll give you one. Go in the dining room and you'll see Mr. Red, White and Blue himself!"

CHAPTER XV

THE UNDERGROUND RIVER

THE young twins peered eagerly into the dining room.

"I see him!" Flossie exclaimed.

Nearby two men were having breakfast. One wore a red shirt, blue slacks and had white hair.

"Are you Mr. Red, White and Blue?" Freddie asked him as the twins stepped up to the table.

"I guess I am," the man said, looking down at his clothes and laughing.

"And I," added his companion, "must be Mr. Green, Yellow and Brown." He had dark hair and was wearing a yellow shirt with green slacks.

"And you're the twin detectives, I'll bet," said the first man. "You've done such a good job, I'd like to give you a treat. My friend and I are going to play golf. Would you like a short ride in our golf carts?"

"That would be fun!" said Flossie. "May I sit with you, Mr. Red, White and Blue?"

"You sure can."

The men gathered up their clubs and took the children to the green outside the inn. The two carts separated for a little tour.

Presently Freddie said, "Whee! Look at that ball go!"

"But it landed in a bad place," said Mr. Green, Yellow and Brown. "It's in the woods."

"Let's help them find the ball," said Freddie, and the cart whizzed to the spot. The little boy jumped out and began to hunt.

"Here it is!" he called out. "By this tree!" Freddie had learned from his father never to touch a golf ball which had been hit.

The player and his caddy hurried over. "Well, thanks a lot, sonny. You have sharp eyes."

Freddie grinned and ran back to the cart. When he returned to the inn, Flossie was already waiting in the lobby. They were just in time to meet the rest of the family and set off for the rehearsal.

Later Mr. Bobbsey let the twins off at the Culver house, then drove on to an appointment.

"Hi!" called Sally Ann from the upper porch. "Come on up! We have something to show you!"

The twins went in the open front door and upstairs. Jay was at a table with a lot of colored papers laid out before him.

"What are you doing?" Bert asked.

"Getting out our signal flags," Sally Ann replied.

"Like the flag of truce?" asked Freddie.

"No. These are International Alphabet Flags," Jay replied. "There are more than forty of them. Each one stands for a letter of the alphabet, and there are pennants for the numbers from zero to nine. At first we used them just for fun, but now even Mother and Daddy sometimes leave messages this way."

"We have some special flags we made up ourselves," said Sally Ann.

"What's this?" asked Nan, pointing to a white arrow on a black flag.

"That means GO," said Sally Ann. She held up an orange flag with a black arrow on it.

"This means COME. We were just getting ready to put up a welcome sign for you," said Sally Ann, "but you came too soon."

"Here's your flag." Jay pointed to a white rectangle with two tall stick figures and two small stick figures drawn on it in blue.

"That's Nan and Bert and Freddie and me," said Flossie.

"I'd like to have a copy of that flag code," said Bert.

"I'll give you mine," said Jay. "Sally Ann and I know it by heart. We gave it to the Townsends too," he added gloomily. "We were having fun with them for a while."

"You'll be friends again," said Nan, "when the mystery's solved."

"I never knew you could talk with flags," put in Flossie.

"Flags do a lot of important jobs," Jay replied. "Red pennants are flown at shore stations to warn boatmen of storms. The flags for hurricane warnings are huge—eight feet square!"

"And the American flag reminds us that we are one nation—lots of different people—but still one nation," said Nan.

Just then Mrs. Culver called from below. "Children! Come here! Hurry!"

As they ran downstairs, she met them at the foot of the stairs.

"I have to leave right away," she said and explained that she had just received a call from her aunt in Yorktown, who had been taken ill. "I'll stay with her until the doctor gets there. Sally Ann, make sandwiches for lunch, dear. Daddy's gone fishing, but you'll be okay, I'm sure. Just don't do anything dangerous."

"We won't," Sally Ann promised.

"There are ice-pops in the freezer for dessert," Mrs. Culver said, then hurried out the front door. In a minute they heard her drive away.

When the six had eaten lunch and tidied the kitchen, they set off for the Red Farm.

"I've been thinking," said Bert, "that if we find the entrance to the underground river, we might need another canoe. I think we should borrow Mr. Barnes's."

The others agreed. Nan, Sally Ann, Jay and Flossie turned back, got the tandem and pedaled to the rabbit man's house. Bert and Freddie went to search for the secret entrance. When they reached the stream no one was in sight.

"It's shallow here," said Bert. "Let's wade in close to the hill."

Barefooted, the boys made their way over slippery rocks toward the overhanging willows. Moving the light boughs aside, Bert ducked under and Freddie followed. Soon they were beneath a low roof of green boughs. Straight ahead was the rocky hillside.

"This is a dead end," Freddie declared.

"Maybe not," said his brother. He had noticed that the stream bed sloped downward and the water flowed faster around the hill.

"Come on!" Bert urged. Holding onto the rocky surface, he made his way around until he saw a large crack.

"You were right," said Freddie. "This whole end is split off from the hill."

The boys went through the wide opening and saw a shallow band of gravel. Bert noted scrape marks in it.

"Those could have been made by a canoe," he said. "Let's keep going down the stream bed."

Stepping off the gravel bar, the boys found the water up to Freddie's knees. They waded toward a curtain of willow boughs. Suddenly the slope became steeper, and the rush of water knocked both boys off their feet and swept them through the curtain of leaves.

Straight ahead was the low, black mouth of the underground river!

Bert shot through the rocky opening, but managed to grasp the side and hang on with one arm.

"Help!" Freddie gasped, and his brother caught him.

"Hang on to my belt!" Bert cried, struggling to his feet. By holding onto rocks and low-hanging branches he made his way back up the slippery slope against the rushing water.

Frightened, Freddie hung on tightly, slipping and sliding behind his brother. Soon they splashed out into the open stream. Soaked and breathless, they flopped on the bank. By the time the other children appeared carrying the canoe over their heads, the boys' light clothing had dried.

Excitedly they reported their discovery.

"Let's get the other canoe and go in," said Bert.

"Right!" Jay agreed. "Come on!"

"Wait!" said Sally Ann. "We promised Mother not to do anything dangerous."

"I don't think it's dangerous," Bert replied. "The water up to the entrance is fast but not very deep. As long as we're in boats we'll be okay. The underground river itself can't be very rough or the intruder wouldn't come and go that way so often."

"It sounds okay," said Jay. "If the trip gets bad we can turn back."

"But what about the monster?" Flossie spoke up. "We don't want to meet him."

"Help!" Freddie gasped

"I don't think we will," said Jay. "We never see or hear him until sundown."

"Besides," added Nan, "there are six of us."

Under Bert's leadership they maneuvered the canoes to the gravel bar. "I'll go first with Sally Ann," he said. "Flossie can ride between us."

"Okay, and Freddie'll go with Jay and me," said Nan.

Moments later the first canoe sped through the willow curtain and down into the dark mouth of the river. The second followed close behind.

"Ooh, it's dark in here!" said Flossie.

"Hold this light," Bert suggested. He handed her his waterproof pocket flashlight.

"You can do the same, Freddie," said Jay, giving the little boy his light.

The young twins flicked the beams. They were in a rocky tunnel with shining black water before them. In a short time the stream bed leveled off and the current became slow.

"It's shallow," said Bert. His voice echoed weirdly. "I can touch bottom with my paddle."

"Look!" exclaimed Flossie. The beam of her light showed a niche in the wall. "Something black's in there!"

"It looks like cloth," said Nan as Freddie also shone his beam into the opening.

Bert maneuvered his canoe closer. Sally Ann reached in and lifted out the black material.

"It's a cape!" she exclaimed, holding it up.

"And look what was under it!" said Freddie. "A lanthorn!"

Bert lifted the old iron lantern from the opening and examined it. "This is from Williamsburg," he said.

"So is the cape," said Sally Ann. "It's part of a hostess costume." She peered at the name tape. "Somebody inked the name out of this," she said, "and put in the initials P. W."

The children looked at each other in amazement. They all understood. Long Arms and the mysterious intruder were the same person!

"What about the monster?" asked Flossie. "Is that Long Arms too, or somebody else or what?"

Before anyone could answer, an unearthly howl sounded somewhere ahead of them. The children froze. Once again came the weird noise.

"That was closer," whispered Bert. "Whatever the thing is, it's coming our way!"

CHAPTER XVI

CAUGHT!

"WHAT'LL we do?" whispered Sally Ann in terror.

The next moment the howl echoed again through the tunnel.

"Let's go back," quavered Flossie. "I'm scared."

"The monster'll get us!" said Freddie.

"It can't be a monster," Bert told them. "I think we ought to find out what the thing is."

Nan and the Culvers agreed. Taking the cape and lanthorn with them, the children paddled the two canoes onward.

As they glided forward through the dark tunnel, the howling became louder. With trembling hands the young twins swept the flashlight over the water and the rocky walls.

Suddenly, as they rounded a bend, Flossie's beam found a niche in the wall. In it sat a dog. He opened his mouth, and the strange howl echoed again through the tunnel.

"Blue!" said Bert. "Corny Wiggins' dog!"

"Do you suppose," Nan asked, "that Corny dresses up in black with flapping wings and uses Blue to howl for him?"

"I'll bet you're right," Jay agreed. "It's the odd echo in here that makes Blue sound so terrible."

"I think he's scared," said Flossie as the hound let out another howl. "Here, Blue, come with us! You were naughty to take my pocketbook, but I guess you were just mischievous."

Bert and Sally Ann moved the canoe closer and Flossie coaxed the dog into it.

"You know what this means," said Bert. "If this *is* Blue, Corny must be Long Arms."

The others nodded agreement. "But where is he?" Jay asked.

"Blue isn't wet," said Flossie, putting an arm around the shivering dog, "so he didn't swim here. Corny must have brought him in a boat."

"Then he left him and went away," said Bert.

"How mean!" Nan exclaimed.

"Let's go ahead," put in Jay. "Maybe we can find Corny. I'm not scared of him."

"Neither am I," the others chorused.

The paddlers went on and soon the tunnel widened. The canoes scraped on the sandy bottom. Straight ahead they could see daylight through a low opening.

The children stepped out and dragged the two boats aside. Under a rock ledge they spotted an old canoe.

"That must be Corny's," said Nan quietly.

Meanwhile Blue had dashed through the opening.

"Let's follow him!" Bert urged.

Quickly the six children put on their sandals and started after him. Creeping under low-hanging willow boughs, they stepped out into a sandy cove facing a wide brown river.

"The James," whispered Sally Ann.

Bert pointed to his right. There stood a small wooden shack with a funny-looking chimney made of tin pipe.

"That might be Corny's place," Nan whispered. "Do you think he's home?"

"He may be," her twin replied. "I think Jay and Sally Ann had better go for the police. The rest of us will do our best to keep him here until they come back."

"We're probably not far from the Colonial Highway," said Jay. "We'll flag down a motorist and get help."

The next moment Blue barked loudly. Quickly the children crouched among some high reeds.

The door of the shack opened and a man with a long, pale face and a sagging chin looked out. It was Corny Wiggins. His eyes widened when he saw the dog. "How did you get here?" he asked. "I left you behind to scare those kids off!"

As the hound trotted into the shack, the man took a long, slow look around the cove. Then he shrugged and went inside again.

"We'll go now," whispered Jay. "Be careful!"

The two Culvers slipped away into the high marsh grass.

"Let's sneak up to the cabin," said Nan, "and see what he's doing."

"Whatever it is," Bert replied, "we must keep him from getting away."

"His car should be around here some place," Nan remarked.

"Right," said Bert. He thought a moment, then gave special instructions to the younger twins.

"We'll do our best," said Freddie. He and Flossie disappeared into the brush.

Nan and Bert crouched low and hurried across the sand to the side of the shack. Cautiously they listened. Not hearing a sound, they peered in the window.

Corny was standing by a wooden table throwing things into a battered suitcase. The twins' eyes grew wide as they recognized stolen property all over the room.

The thief was fitting the violin into the bag next to the wig. Flossie's little purse was on the floor with Bud's compass and a heap of artifacts. The two rabbits were in their cage in a corner behind a box of key chains and some green glass vases, and the binoculars. On a cot lay a colonial costume with blue breeches.

As Corny glanced up, the children ducked down. *Had he seen them?*

The next moment they heard the door open. Be-

fore they could move, Long Arms was beside
them.

"So! Spying on me, eh?" he said angrily. "Inside! March!"

Remembering their plan to delay the thief's
getaway, the twins did not try to run away.

"You ought to be ashamed of yourself, stealing
all this stuff," said Bert, as they entered the shack.

"Never mind about that," snapped Corny.
"How did you ever find that underground river?"

"How did you?" countered Bert.

"I was exploring the cove one day and spotted
the opening," the thief replied. "I decided to
follow the stream."

"Weren't you afraid?" asked Nan.

"Course not!" replied the man scornfully. "But
Blue was. He howled all the way."

"Once I heard voices," Corny went on. "The
Culver kids were talking outside the crack in the
hill. They said the howls sounded like a monster."
He grinned. "That gave me the idea of taking
Blue along each time and using the cape to play
monster. I even got two flashlights with green
bulbs in 'em for eyes. I figured I'd scare everybody away from that farm."

"What for?" asked Bert.

"Well, I don't know what kind of interesting
old junk I might find there, and I didn't want any
interference while I was poking around." He
smiled slyly. "After you found the trash pit for
me, I went oftener."

"Spying on me, eh? Inside! March!"
the man said angrily

"I guess you rigged up that bucket in the tree and ran poor old Daisy up the road and hung a sign on her," said Nan.

"Right," Corny said. As he talked he had been sticking other objects into the suitcase. "Have you found that flag yet?" he questioned.

"How did you know about that?" asked Nan. She guessed the answer, but knew they had to keep Corny talking.

"I was up in the tree," he replied, "and heard you talking about it."

"And you eavesdropped on the terrace outside the dining room," Nan added.

"Right," said the thief cheerfully, closing the suitcase.

The twins wondered whether the Culvers had found a policeman yet.

"Too bad about the flag," Corny went on as he threw things into a duffel bag. "I hoped to find it. In fact, I was willing to risk a daylight search for it, but when I heard your voices in the tunnel, I figured I'd better get back here and clear out. It'd only be a matter of time till you found my place." He glanced nervously out the window.

"What were you going to do with the flag if you found it?" Nan asked.

"Sell it," Corny replied, "same as the old stuff I dug up at the Red Farm. I'll bet Colonial Williamsburg would have paid me good for all of it." He scowled at the children. "I can't do that now, thanks to you."

"How did you get started as Long Arms?" asked Bert.

"It was easy. I just snitched the colonial costume and the waiter's coat." The thief explained that he had taken one piece of clothing at a time over a period of several months. Each article had come from a different person.

"People thought the stuff had been lost in the laundry or mislaid," he said with a grin.

"You were the man who didn't answer the day I called to you from the pillory, weren't you?" Bert asked.

Corny nodded. "And I was the fellow in the grape arbor," he added with a sly grin. "I bet you'll never guess where Blue was."

"Under the basket," said the twins together.

Corny sighed. "I might have known you'd guess."

"I'll just take my sister's purse, thank you," said Nan, picking it up from the floor. "And Bud's compass, too."

"I never took the purse," said Corny, looking very innocent. "Blue did that, and I just carried it home for him."

"You ought to be ashamed, blaming it on him," said Nan. "He's only a dog and doesn't know right from wrong."

Corny blinked. "Never mind the lectures," he said. "I've had a hard life. My real name is Percy Cornelius Wiggins. That's enough to make anybody go bad."

"No, it isn't," said Bert.

Corny slung the full duffel bag over his shoulder. "What about Blue?" Nan asked quickly. "Were you going to leave him in that tunnel?"

"He was in no danger," said Corny. "The water's shallow. He'd have come out after a while. But he hates to get his feet wet."

"What about the rabbits?" put in Bert, trying to delay the thief.

"Can't take 'em," he replied regretfully.

Corny opened the door and flung his suitcase onto the grass. Blue ran out and stood beside it.

"I'm going to lock you kids in," Corny said with a grin. "By the time you get out, I'll be through the woods and gone."

As the twins tried to grab him, he slipped out and slammed the door. They heard a padlock snap shut.

"Quick! The window!" said Nan. She ran over and tried to open it. It was stuck tight!

"No wonder he figured he'd have time," said Bert.

Nan took off her sandal and banged on the frame. Then as her brother tried again, the window creaked upward. In a twinkling the twins had climbed out.

They ran as quietly as they could into the woods. From the crackling in the brush ahead they were able to follow the fleeing man and his dog.

Suddenly they reached a dirt road. Parked by the side of it was Corny's old jalopy.

As the thief hurled his baggage into the back seat, two policemen burst from the trees with Sally Ann and Jay at their heels.

"Halt!" cried the officers. But Corny leaped into the driver's seat and Blue jumped in beside him.

"He's getting away!" cried Sally Ann. "Stop him!"

CHAPTER XVII

EXCITING CLUE

THE thief turned the ignition key and started his motor just as the young twins ran out from behind a clump of brush.

"You've got four flat tires!" Freddie cried.

"Okay, Wiggins," said the first policeman as they raced up to the jalopy. "You're under arrest."

The second officer was close behind him and in a twinkling Corny was out of the car and handcuffed.

"I didn't have a flat," he said in bewilderment. "What happened?"

"Freddie and I let the air out of all four tires," said Flossie. "Bert told us how to do it."

"I figured his car had to be parked somewhere near the shack," said Bert. He grinned and smiled at his younger brother and sister. "Good work."

"Those twins again!" cried Corny miserably. "I was doing great until they came along."

"Jay and Sally Ann helped too," said Nan

quickly. "It's a good thing you came back with the police when you did," she told the Culvers.

"We were lucky," Jay replied. "Just as we reached the highway, we saw a patrol car coming and flagged it down."

Bert told the officers about the loot in the shack. The first policeman, a powerfully built man with dark hair, had been speaking quietly into a walkie-talkie.

"I've radioed for another car," he said. "I'll take this fellow to headquarters. I'd like you two to go along." He nodded to Bert and Nan.

"I want to see that shack you mentioned," said the second officer. He was a tall, broad-shouldered young man with sandy hair.

"Sally Ann and Jay can show you," said Nan. "By the way, Mr. Wiggins," she added, "Lieutenant Mercer has your lucky horseshoe. My brother found it in the maze."

Corny shook his head gloomily. "My luck certainly ran out the day you came to town."

The dog woofed and rubbed against Corny's leg.

"Poor Blue," he said softly. "I don't know what's going to become of you."

The children felt sorry for the hound. "Never mind," Sally Ann spoke up. "I'm sure Mother will let us keep him for you."

Corny brightened. "Thank you very much," he said.

"And I hope you'll never be a bad man again," said Flossie.

"I won't," said Corny earnestly. "I've learned my lesson. When I'm free again I'll go to work."

"Come along," said the first officer. "Our patrol car is around the bend in the road. We'll take a shortcut through the woods the way we came."

He led the prisoner off with Nan and Bert. Holding Blue by the collar, the other children guided the second policeman to the shack. Then they took him to the underground river and gave him the cape and lanthorn from the canoe.

"You have done a fine job," the officer said warmly. "Lieutenant Mercer will be pleased to know the case is cleared up."

He hurried back to the dirt road to wait for the other patrol car. The children got into the canoes. Shivering and howling, Blue rode next to Flossie.

When they reached the Culver house, Bert and Nan were already there and Mr. Bobbsey had arrived. Everyone knew of the capture.

"Congratulations!" Mrs. Culver, who had returned, hugged the new arrivals. "But I'd have worried if I had known what you were doing."

"Well, everything turned out okay," Mr. Culver said, beaming. "You children were right all along about the intruder. We should have listened to you."

"Let's call the Townsends right away," said Nan. "When they hear about Corny Wiggins, they'll stop blaming us for all the mischief."

"They're on an overnight hike with their parents," Mrs. Culver told her, "and won't be home until tomorrow morning. Their mother told me about it last week."

"Then I'll leave them a note to meet us at the dig site tomorrow after the pageant," said Jay.

"Make it at noon," said Mrs. Culver. "And invite all of them here. I think we should have a picnic to celebrate our detectives' success."

"But we haven't found the flag yet," said Bert, frowning.

"No, and I'm afraid you'll have to do it soon or not at all," said Mr. Bobbsey. "You know Mother is coming tonight. We'll be going home in a few days. She may be at the hotel now," he added, glancing at his watch. "We'd better find out."

The twins made arrangements to meet the Culvers after the pageant. Then Mr. Bobbsey drove the children back to the inn. They hurried into the lobby.

"Mommy!" cried Flossie. She raced toward a slender, pretty young woman in a pink suit.

Mrs. Bobbsey scooped the little girl up in her arms. The other twins were close behind and everyone was hugged and kissed and hugged again.

"Mommy, Mommy, we solved the mystery!" cried Freddie.

"And we bought a present for you," said Flossie at the same time.

"And caught Long Arms!" Nan exclaimed.

"Oh, please!" said their mother, laughing and holding up her hands. "One at a time!"

"We'll hear all about everything at dinner," said Mr. Bobbsey firmly. "Now, children, please get ready and report to the dining room. Scoot!"

An hour later all the news had been exchanged and Mrs. Bobbsey had opened her gift.

"I just love the seeds!" she said. "You are very thoughtful children. And clever ones, too, to solve the mystery. I can't wait to see you in the pageant."

Next day at ten o'clock sharp the twins reported to the courthouse where the girls were to dress. The boys went across the street to the guardhouse.

"I just love my costume," said Flossie. "I wish I could keep it."

She wore a blue dress with a wide skirt and a frilly white butterfly cap. Nan's outfit was pink.

Both boys had on their tricorn hats. Freddie wore blue breeches with a white full-sleeved shirt. Bert had a red coat, matching pants and a yellow waistcoat. White stockings and black shoes with big buckles completed their outfits.

By eleven o'clock the twins were in line for the opening parade. First came a tall actor dressed as George Washington. He rode a large white horse. Then a group of old-fashioned musicians called The Band of Musick followed with drums and brass instruments. Next came the militiamen with banners and drums and finally the schoolchildren in their colonial costumes.

As the music boomed out, the paraders walked briskly through the crowded streets to the palace. Here they were joined by a carriage with performers in it dressed as the governor and his lady. The procession marched on to the green in front of the palace. The twins took their places between George Washington on his horse and Daniel's group of fifers and drummers.

The governor stood up in the carriage and used a microphone to announce each group. One school had sent thirteen children who sang a song they had written. From another came ten who danced a colonial minuet.

"They're all so good," whispered Freddie.

"Shh!" said Bert. "We're next."

The twins held their breath, then heard the governor announce the names of the children from Lakeport School.

The militia boys beat a roll on the drums as the four children ran to the microphone in the center of the green.

"Our flag," announced Flossie. With music in the background, each twin spoke one verse of their poem. Then together they recited the last part:

> Be proud of the flag
> Of the U. S. A.
> And pledge allegiance
> Every day.
> Fly it high
> From East to West
> The Stars and Stripes
> Stand for the best.

As everyone applauded, the girls swept curtsies

and the boys bowed. Then they ran to their places. Just then someone whistled shrilly and the white horse neighed and reared. The children screamed, as the frightened animal began plunging.

"Watch out!" yelled Daniel. He pulled Nan back as the hoofs just missed her. With the help of several militiamen, "George Washington" managed to calm the horse.

"I told them not to use Big Boy," Daniel said to Bert. "He's always nervous in crowds. They should have used Little Boy. He's steady."

As Bert thought over what his friend had said, he suddenly had an idea. If Little Boy was a horse's name, why not Little Gray? Maybe John's Little Gray was a horse—the hobbyhorse which the boy was riding in the picture!

The pageant came to an end as the Color Guard unfurled Old Glory and the band played "The Star Spangled Banner." Everyone joined in to sing the National Anthem. It was a thrilling moment.

As the crowd broke up and started to move away, Bert quickly told his idea to the other twins.

Nan clasped her hands in excitement. "Oh, I'll bet that's right!"

"But where can the hobbyhorse be?" asked Flossie.

For a moment no one answered, then Nan said, "I think I know!"

"Where?" chorused the others.

"In Mr. Barnes's shed. You remember the label pasted on the little desk? It said that this was *one*

The frightened animal began plunging

of the toys given by the Redfield family to the Barnes children. I'll bet they also gave them the hobbyhorse."

"Let's get dressed and go look for it!" said Flossie.

In fifteen minutes they had met their parents and the Culvers on the courthouse steps. Quickly Bert told his idea.

"You might have something there," said Mr. Bobbsey, "but I wouldn't count too much on it. You know, Mr. Barnes may not have that horse anymore—if he ever had it."

"Besides," Mrs. Culver added, "you promised to meet the Townsend children at noon."

"Oh, phooey! That's right. We forgot!" Freddie exclaimed.

"We'll tell them about it," said Bert, "and we can look for it together after lunch. After all, they want to find the flag too."

When the two families arrived at the Culver house in their cars, the children hastened to the Red Farm. As they crossed the clearing, the Townsends ran out from the woods toward them.

"Don't step over that line!" bellowed Bud.

Reaching the dig site, the other children saw a clothesline stretched along the ground.

"Come on, Bud, forget it," called Bert. "We have something to tell you."

The twins and the Culvers stepped over the line. *Sssssss!* Thin streams of cold water whipped across their faces!

CHAPTER XVIII

SURPRISES!

"WATER pistols!" exclaimed Bert, ducking.

"That's to pay you back for all your mean tricks!" yelled Bud as he and Phil sent another spray of water from their toys.

"Cut it out!" called Jay as he and the others drew back. "We want to tell you something important."

"Forget it," Phil replied. Terry stood with her brothers, but did not use her water pistol.

Bert spoke up. "Let Freddie go out with a flag of truce. Then they'll have to talk to us."

"Good idea," said Jay. He reached into his pocket and pulled out a clean handkerchief. "Here, this can be our white flag."

"Tie it to a stick," Bert suggested. In a few moments the flag was ready.

"Tell them we want to parley," Sally Ann told Freddie as he marched forward.

For a moment there was no sound from the opposite side. Then Phil said, "What do you want?"

"To par—ley!" Freddie replied.

At first there was no answer. Then Bud called grudgingly, "Okay."

The three Townsends waited at the clothesline as the other children came up to them.

"We have news," said Bert and quickly told about the capture of Long Arms Wiggins.

"I'm surprised you didn't hear about it," Sally Ann spoke up when the Townsends stared suspiciously.

"We've been on a hike," Terry said. "We didn't have a radio or anything, and we just got back and found your note."

"I don't know what you're up to," said Bud, "but I'm sure it's some kind of trick."

"So am I," Phil added, scowling.

"I'm not," Terry said. Her brothers turned to her in surprise. "I don't think they're really mean. After all, they did pull me out of the thorns. I think they're telling the truth."

"We are, Terry," Nan assured her. "Please don't be angry any more," she told the boys. "We didn't play any of those tricks. Corny Wiggins did."

"You can ask anybody in Williamsburg," said Jay. "Everybody knows about how the Bobbseys caught Long Arms and he confessed everything."

For a few moments the Townsend boys looked uncomfortable.

"Well, I'm sorry then," said Bud finally.

"So am I," Phil put in.

"So am I," said Terry.

"We shouldn't have gotten sore," Bud confessed.

"I got mad, too," said Jay, "and I'm sorry. Bert told me to cool it."

"That's what we all should have done," Bud added.

"Never mind," Sally Ann put in. "You're invited to a picnic at our house. My mother is calling your parents and Uncle El to come, too."

The Townsends brightened. "That's great," said Bud.

Phil hurried to the woods and brought out Daisy, who had been waiting there. As the children trooped across the Red Farm, leading the horse, Nan told the Townsends Bert's idea about the flag.

"We'll help you search for it," said Terry eagerly.

"I'm glad nobody's mad any more," said Flossie happily as she skipped along next to Terry.

When the children reached the Culvers' yard, the picnic tables were laden with bowls of salad and fruit, steaming baked beans and baskets of buns. Hamburgers and hot dogs sizzled on the outdoor grill.

While they ate the delicious food, the twins and the Culver children told the guests the full story of the capture of Long Arms Wiggins.

"And now we want to find the flag," added Bert. He explained about the hobbyhorse. "Do you think it's in your shed?" he asked Mr. Barnes.

"I don't know. You'll just have to look," said Uncle El.

"Let's all go," said Mr. Culver.

"I'll take the nine detectives in my pickup," said Mr. Barnes. "The rest of you follow in cars."

While the three mothers put the food away, the children drove off with their friend. When they reached his yard, they made their way into the crowded shed and began the search. By the time their parents had arrived, they had come out dusty and hot but without the hobbyhorse.

"Have you searched everywhere?" asked Mr. Bobbsey.

"Yes," the nine searchers replied.

"No, wait!" exclaimed Bert, snapping his fingers. "Jay, remember when we climbed up to get down the tandem?" His friend nodded. "I saw a big canvas bag way in the back between the rafters and the roof."

"Do you recall what's in it, El?" asked Mr. Culver.

The rabbit keeper shook his head. "I have no idea. I just told the moving men to store all that old stuff in the shed."

"Come on, Jay," said Bert. "Let's go up and get it down and see what it is!"

The boys climbed onto the tall chest of drawers and into the rafters. Carefully they inched their way over the wide beams toward the bag in the shadows under the roof. When they reached it, Bert stepped to the next beam.

"Easy now," he said. "We'll have to back up and pull it along the rafters."

The bag was heavy, but they managed to maneuver it to the front of the shed.

"Here it comes," said Bert.

He and Jay dropped the burden to Phil and Bud, then swung themselves down.

"Open it quick!" cried Freddie as everyone gathered around the dusty bag.

With eager fingers Nan untied the cord which was fastened around the top. Sally Ann and Flossie helped her pull out bundles of rags. Under them was a faded gray hobbyhorse!

"We've found it!" cried the young twins. Everyone exclaimed in excitement and delight as the girls hugged each other.

"Look inside it!" urged Terry.

Carefully the boys took the old toy from the sack and set it on its rockers. One glass eye was missing, but it still had four legs, a rope tail and mane and a faded red saddle.

"I wonder how Mary Redfield opened it," said Mrs. Bobbsey.

"Maybe she split a seam, took out some stuffing, put the box inside and then sewed it up again," suggested Mrs. Townsend.

"I don't see any outside stitches," said Nan.

"Maybe the saddle comes off," Flossie suggested.

"I think it does!" exclaimed Sally Ann. "It has straps which go around the body."

The girls tipped the horse and Nan started to open the buckles, but the rotting leather bands fell apart. The saddle dropped off.

"The seam *is* split!" exclaimed Mrs. Culver. Tufts of old stuffing stuck out of the horse's back.

With trembling fingers, Nan began to remove it. In a moment the black edge of an iron box appeared. Nan pulled it out and with Bert's help opened the lid.

"It's the flag!" cried Freddie as the red and white stripes appeared.

Very gently the older twins lifted out the banner and unfolded it. In the blue field was a circle of twelve stars around one in the middle.

For a moment no one spoke, then Flossie murmured, "Oooh, it's bee-yoo-ti-ful!"

"It's almost as good as new," said Mrs. Culver quietly. "Only a bit faded."

"And to think it was up in my shed all the time," said Mr. Barnes.

"But we mustn't keep it exposed to the air very long," said Mr. Culver quickly. "Remember this is very old and fragile."

As the twins carefully folded the flag again and placed it in the box, he said he would take it to the Archaeology Department for safekeeping.

"Wouldn't it be great if the old Red House could be reconstructed?" said Bert.

"And refurnished," added Nan. "The artifacts we found could be displayed."

"The flag could be shown there too," said her twin, "with the hobbyhorse and the little desk—if Mr. Barnes would let you have them."

"Count me in!" said the rabbit keeper heartily.

"It's a fine idea!" exclaimed Mr. Townsend. "We could do a lot of it ourselves. You're an archaeologist, Ed, and I'm a mason. How about it?"

"Oh, please, Daddy!" chorused Jay and Sally Ann.

"We'll all help," promised Bud, and Phil and Terry nodded.

"It'll take a lot of time and some money," said Mr. Culver, "but I think we can get help. It's a deal!"

The men shook hands and everyone cheered.

"Oh, it sounds like such fun!" said Freddie. "I wish we could be here."

His mother smiled. "We must go home soon, dear, but maybe we'll come back someday."

During the next three days the Bobbseys enjoyed Williamsburg and the farm with their friends. On the last morning they met in the lobby of the inn to say good-by. The girls hugged each other, and everyone promised to write.

As they walked out the door, the Bobbseys stopped short in amazement. Standing in a big circle around the porch were all the workers of Williamsburg in their costumes! The clock shop man stepped forward.

"We have brought you Bobbsey twins a gift,"

"We want you Bobbseys to leave Williamsburg
in real eighteenth century style"

he announced, "for capturing Long Arms. The cabinet maker made it, but it's from all of us."

The men brought forward four life-sized dummy boards of the twins themselves.

"Those will be sent to your home," said Mrs. Culver with a smile. "We have ordered another set for the Red House. When it is restored," she added, "you twins will be placed by the fireplace in the dining room. In that way you will never really leave Williamsburg!"

Before the astonished children could speak, Daniel and Lieutenant Mercer stepped forward, holding up a Grand Union flag. "This is for you, too," said the boy, grinning. "We'll send it to you."

As he spoke, a two-horse carriage bowled up to the inn.

"We want you to leave Williamsburg in real eighteenth century style," said Lieutenant Mercer. "A special limousine with your bags in it is waiting at the Information Center to take you to the airport."

At last the surprised family could speak. After saying happy thanks they climbed into the carriage.

"So many surprises!" exclaimed Freddie.

"There's one more!" said Sally Ann, her eyes twinkling.

"The last is from us," added Terry.

Waving and calling good-by, the Bobbseys were driven off. Fifteen minutes later they were in the big limousine. As it slowed down to pass the Culver farm, they saw signal flags fluttering outside the porch. Nan read them.

"Good-by Bobbseys!"

Moments later they reached the Townsend house and saw the rest of the message in flags flying from their roof. *"Come back again!"* read Bert.

"Oh, I hope we can," cried Flossie, " 'cause Williamsburg was full of such 'citing surprises!"

THE PLEDGE OF ALLEGIANCE

I pledge allegiance to the Flag of the United States of America and to the Republic for which it stands; one Nation under God, indivisible, with liberty and justice for all.

Who wrote the Pledge?

Francis Bellamy. He was a member of the staff of *Youth's Companion,* published in Boston. This magazine was first to print the Pledge on September 8, 1892.

Why was it written?

That year was the 4th centennial of the discovery of America by Columbus, and President Benjamin Harrison had called for patriotic exercises in the schools to celebrate the event.

Who was first to speak the Pledge?

It was recited by millions of American schoolchildren on Columbus Day, 1892.

Has the Pledge changed?

Yes. In the beginning we pledged allegiance to "my Flag." In 1923 the National Flag Conference changed this to "the Flag of the United States" and in 1924 to "the Flag of the United States of America." In 1954 Congress added the words "under God."

How should we give the Pledge?

Always face the flag and stand up straight with the right hand over the heart, horizontal to the arm, fingers together. When the pledge is over, lower the arm to the side.

SOME RULES FOR DISPLAYING THE FLAG

1. It is the universal custom to display the flag only from sunrise to sunset on buildings or on stationary flagstaffs in the open. However, the flag may be displayed at night upon special occasions when it is desired to produce a patriotic effect.
2. The flag should be hoisted briskly and lowered ceremoniously.
3. The flag should not be displayed on days when the weather is inclement.
4. The flag should be displayed during school days in or near every schoolhouse.
5. The flag, when carried in a procession with another flag or flags, should be either on the flag's own right, or, if there is a line of other flags, in the center of that line.
6. The flag of the United States of America, when it is displayed with another flag against a wall from crossed staffs, should be on the right, the flag's own right, and its staff should be in front of the staff of the other flag.

7. The flag should never be used as drapery of any sort whatever.
8. The flag should never be used for advertising purposes in any manner whatsoever.
9. The flag should never be displayed with the union down save as a signal of dire distress.

From: *Our Flag,* U. S. House Document 165. Page 168.